BREAKING THE Ice

WHITNEY DINEEN

Made in the United States. July 2024

Print ISBN: 979-8-9912328-0-7
E-book ASIN: B0D8D3YV2Z

https://whitneydineen.com/newsletter/

33 Partners Publishing

Map of the Town

CHAPTER ONE

Zach

I've learned a lot of things from being a billionaire in my thirties, but so far, the most essential is that you can't have thin skin. *Everyone* wants a piece of you and when you're not giving them the time or attention they think they deserve, they set out to tear you down. Case in point, Yolanda Simms, the entertainment reporter for KBIZ and the most annoyingly fame-seeking woman it has ever been my displeasure to know.

Yolanda and I went out three times, which is a record for me as I barely have a minute for myself. Given my busy schedule, you might be wondering why I would spend my precious free time with such a person. When I first asked her out, I didn't see her for who she truly was. I may have also had a hidden agenda.

I'd recently been called out by a national tabloid for not putting my money where my mouth was. As in, they didn't think I donated enough to charity. And while supposedly no press is bad press, I really don't like people thinking of me the way I was being portrayed.

I figured if I wined and dined Yolanda—who had previously flirted with me outrageously every time she saw me—she might spread the word that I was a decent guy. Self-serving? Yes. But I'm not the villain the press would have you think I am, and I wanted a chance to prove it.

Unfortunately, Yolanda got ahead of herself regarding our friendship and decided to announce on air that she and I were in an exclusive and committed relationship. As we had never so much as kissed, I took exception to her declaration.

"Zachary!" my assistant Anabelle yells out. Before I can ask her what she wants, she says, "Your brother is on line three."

I have five brothers, so I ask, "Which one?"

Instead of answering, I overhear her tell someone else, "Mr. Hart has no comment on Ms. Simms' allegations." Great, another day fending off the aftermath of Yolanda's interview on *The View*. She told Whoopi Goldberg I was an egomaniacal alpha-male.

I hesitantly reach over to the landline on my desk. "This is Zach."

"Hey, big bro," my younger twin says. In my mind's eye, I see his lopsided grin, which, even though we're fraternal twins, is remarkably like my own. MacElroy, aka Mac, is four minutes younger than me and has four times the personality. "It's starting to look like you're wading through a herd of cows in a rainy field."

"What does that even mean, Mac?" My brother recently bought a sustainable farm in Oregon and his metaphors have taken on a rural sort of charm.

"Where there are cows there are cow pies. Need I explain that a rainy field full of heifers is full of wet ..."

"Manure. Got it." *Gross.*

"Why don't you set the world straight and tell them the majority of your charitable donations are given anonymously?" he wants to know. The man definitely cuts to the chase.

"You do know the definition of anonymous, don't you?" I condescendingly inquire.

"Yes, Zach. What I don't know is why you don't just come clean about what a good guy you are."

"Because if I bragged about doing good deeds, they wouldn't feel like good deeds," I tell him for the hundredth time.

Shifting in my chair, I stare out of my home office window onto Wilshire Boulevard below. You'd think all the short skirts and tanned legs would be one of the benefits of living in Southern California. Yet no matter how good the view is, wealthy Beverly Hills women are not my type. They're simply too high mainte- nance, not to mention too self-involved.

"I'm just saying…"

"Let it go, Mac." Removing my feet from the edge of my giant mahogany desk, I ask, "Did you call for any other reason than to bust my butt about Yolanda? Because if not, I have work to do."

"What are you buying today?" he wants to know. "Another office building? A high-rise? *Malibu*?" While I like to have a diver- sified financial portfolio, as a real estate developer, I am obviously partial to buying property.

"I'm giving a speech at Pepperdine," I tell him. Tongue in cheek, I add, "I call it 'One House, New House, Big House, You House.'"

"Ah yes, a nod to your childhood love of Dr. Seuss." Releasing an exaggerated yawn, he asks, "Has anyone ever told you that you're becoming kind of boring?"

"*You* tell me that at least twice a week," I remind him. "Now, why are you calling?"

Instead of putting me out of my misery, he wants to know, "When was the last time you strapped on a pair of skates and played a game?"

"Not since that gong show when Howie Heller whacked my left knee with his stick." Not a coincidence, that also marked the end of my college hockey career.

"Are you serious, man? That was over a decade ago."

"What's your point?"

"The Hart brothers were practically born on the ice!" He's not kidding, either. Our mom went into labor with me and Mac while ice skating—something she most certainly shouldn't have been doing four weeks prior to her due date.

Even without our auspicious start in this world, skating really is in our blood. It's also the only reason we all went to college—go, scholarships! Instead of agreeing with my brother, I grunt, "I don't want another year of physical therapy. Not to mention, my surgeon guaranteed I'd need a knee replacement if I took another hit like that."

"Dude, who *are* you?"

Rolling my eyes, I tell him, "I'm a grown adult who knows when not to take a stupid risk. Now, why did you call?"

He releases a snort of disdain. "Troy and I have a plan to get you out of trouble with the press."

I don't usually pander to the media, but between being called a skinflint, followed by Yolanda's revenge quest to bring me to my knees, I'm seriously starting to worry about my reputation. "I'm listening."

"Troy and Kelly just bought a skating rink in Maple Falls." My oldest brother and his wife live in a small town in Washington state. Buying a rink seems like a reasonable thing to do as all their kids are skaters.

"So?"

"Troy is hoping to get the contract for the Olympic team to train there."

"I guess that makes sense, being that he was on said team back in the day. But why would the Olympics go to a one-horse town like Maple Falls?"

"Why wouldn't they? It's a great little town. There aren't a ton of distractions so everyone can focus on training."

"They only have a few restaurants, two gas stations, a handful of streetlights, and no Costco. They might die of boredom."

"They also have a diner, a hardware store, a bookstore, and a bakery." He hurries to add, "I think there might even be a movie theater."

"A veritable metropolis then," I drawl. "Where would the team stay if they went there? Is Troy going to build a compound?"

"They'll stay at the lodge." Ah, yes, the forty-room hotel my brother bought as an investment. While not the kind of establishment that comes to mind when I think of luxury vacationing—as in, there's no spa and only one restaurant—I suppose I could see a bunch of athletes living there. They wouldn't have to cook or clean, and they could spend their free time zip-lining through the woods on the property.

Endeavoring to bring Mac back to the point of this conversation, I ask, "So, Troy needs cash to update the arena? I'm happy to give it to him, but I can't see that fixing my bad press."

"Nah. The rink is in great shape."

Confused, I walk over to the large picture window in my living room and watch a group of tourists make their way toward Rodeo Drive. My brother continues, "Troy has formed a charity league full of current and retired NHL players, along with some memorable college players. His friend, Angela Davis, started a charity called Happy Horizons Ranch that serves underprivileged kids."

He's got my attention now. "Who are the players and who are they going to compete against?"

"He got Dan Roberts from his Blizzard days, and Dawson Hayes, who used to play with Dan in college. Then there's Copper Montgomery, Noah Beaumont, and Ted 'The Bear' Powell. There are others, but these guys are the real heart of the team."

"That's an impressive group, but I thought Ted was recovering from a nasty knee injury."

My brother explains, "His coach wants him to rest, but he's ready to get back to it. Troy thinks he has what it takes to give it his all for the charity."

"What are the stakes?" I want to know. "When does Troy want to start?"

"I knew you'd be in!" my brother shouts excitedly. "You can take the man off the ice, but you can't take the ice out of the man."

While I'm clearly impressed with the idea, I need to make something clear. "I'm not going back into the trenches, even to help poor kids." My knee aches at the very thought.

"He doesn't want you as a player, he wants you as a backer."

"That I can do."

"Troy talked to Hank up in Ontario. Hank is putting together a Canadian team, and the two teams will play each other. Best out of five wins it for their charity." After being on the gold medal Olympic team, my oldest brother played for the NHL, which is where he met Hank York.

"You know I'm up for anything to help kids."

"Troy wants to make sure families have enough food and clothes. He's even going to teach hockey for kids at his new place."

"How much does he want?" Having grown up wearing a long line of hand-me-downs, I have a soft spot for children in need. So much so, I would gladly hand my brother a blank check.

"He wants you to match all corporate donations up to two million."

I don't hesitate before answering, "Done. What else?"

"He wants you on site for the whole thing. The way the press has been hounding you, he'll have the attention of the world. Which should bring in corporate sponsors out the wazoo."

Even though I'm sick to death of the press, this kind of exposure could do a lot to help me regain my previous reputation. "How long would I have to be in Washington?"

"The team has already been picked and they start arriving next week. Troy figures six weeks ought to do the trick. You can leave for meetings and stuff, you just have to make Maple Falls your base."

Without hesitation, I walk toward the back of my condo and call out, "Belle, I'm leaving town!"

CHAPTER TWO

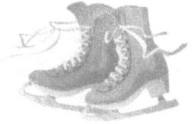

Ellie

"Come on, Brooklyn, you got this!" I cheer as one of my favorite beginners makes her second attempt at a three jump. It's only a one-hundred-and-eighty-degree turn, but to a novice that can feel like you're trying to circle the planet.

As my seven-year-old student's skates leave the ice, her upper body rotates and darn if she doesn't nearly complete a full axel. Unfortunately, her landing isn't quite as successful. She comes down on a wobbly ankle and winds up smack on her bottom. Even though she's got to be in some pain, Brooklyn calls out, "I did it, Ellie! I really did it!" Her smile is as bright as the sun.

Skating over to her, I bend down to check out her leg. "You're a superstar, Brookie!" Her ankle doesn't look too bad, so I gingerly help her to her feet. "Come on, let's get you to the bench."

Kelly Hart, who's been watching from behind the boards, steps over a break in the barrier and hurries to Brooklyn's side. "You did a fantastic job, kiddo!" She brushes her hand over Brookie's box braids. Lifting her phone, she announces, "I got it all on video. Your mom's going to flip when she sees this."

The little girl's look of pride makes my heart clench. Like many of my students, Brooklyn doesn't come from a well-to-do family and her lessons are being funded by Kelly and her husband Troy. "You're the best, Mrs. Hart!"

Kelly shoots her a double thumbs up before pulling me off to the side. While Brooklyn takes off her skates, my boss says, "I have a favor to ask."

"Anything for you." The Harts have singlehandedly kept me in work for the last year since my flower shop closed. They've been super flexible with my schedule too, which means the world to me as I'm my mom's primary caregiver.

Both my mom's health and her income have dwindled significantly since my dad died. As such, I try to stay on top of the upkeep and maintenance at her house. I also make sure she has food in her cupboards and drive her to her various doctor's appointments. Osteoarthritis is no joke and I'm afraid that one of these days, I'm going to have to liquidate her assets so I can afford to put her into an assisted living situation. That day appears to be coming much sooner than I would have ever thought.

Kelly interrupts my thoughts. "My brother-in-law is coming to town, and I was hoping he could stay in the cabin on your mom's property." My parents have a small cottage behind their house that they used to rent out during the summer months. Unfortunately, there have been no takers for five years. While Maple Creek is a fabulous vacation destination, these days most people want more excitement for their money. Therefore, they either stay at the Hawk River Lodge or the Regent Hotel.

"Which brother-in-law?" I demand like I'm questioning her in an espionage case. I'd be fine with any of them except for Zachary. That arrogant man makes me mad just looking at him. All six foot two, wide shouldered, chiseled jaw, and grey-green eyes that resemble a mossy pond ... *Where was I going with this?*

Brushing a wisp of light brown hair aside, Kelly answers, "Zach. I know your mom wants a long-term renter, but I figure while she's waiting, she might as well make a few bucks."

"*Zachary Hart?*" I spit like I've just taken a bite out of a rotten apple. My expression contorts into a look of pure disgust. My inability to control my facial features is the main reason I'm such a horrible poker player. Everyone knows what kind of hand I have just by looking at me.

"You can't possibly hate him so much you'd cut off your nose to spite your face." She gives me one of her famous "talk your way out of that" looks.

I ram my hands into my pockets and turn her logic back on her. "How can I hate him when I don't even know him?"

"I know you think Zach is a stuck-up playboy with too much money and too little compassion." She knows this because I recently told her as much after watching an interview with Yolanda Simms.

"Well, isn't he?" As far as I'm concerned, people like Troy's stinky little stuck-up brat of a brother are the reason we have so many poor people in this country. Zach is a Mr. Moneybags always looking to build his own worth instead of helping others. *How much money does one person need anyway?*

Narrowing her eyes to half-mast, Kelly says, "He's nothing like you think he is."

"That's not what's being said on the news."

My boss's spine straightens. "Yes, well, *they've* got it wrong. Why would you ever believe those yellow journalists over me?"

She's got me there. Not only do I run errands for Kelly and Troy, but I've also taken on the job of their housecleaner, pet sitter, and I occasionally stay with their kids when they're out of town.

Kelly takes my silence for capitulation. "So, you'll talk to your mom about renting him the cottage?"

Out of the corner of my eye, I watch Brooklyn tie her shoes. "I guess so, but you should know the cabin is pretty basic. I'm sure Mr. Fancy Pants will hate it."

"Zach isn't fancy."

I don't believe her for a minute and my left eyebrow arches accordingly. "How long will he be staying there?"

"About two months. He gets here on Friday."

"This Friday? As in, two days from now?" I practically shout. "I'm not sure I'll have time to get it ready by then." In a last-ditch attempt to have nothing to do with the bad boy billionaire of the Hart family, I ask, "Why doesn't he stay at Hawk River Lodge or at your house?"

"Hawk River is housing the hockey players coming to town and Zach doesn't want to be in the middle of so much action." Shrugging her shoulders, she adds, "My house isn't exactly a serene environment." Kelly's got that right. Every time I've been there, her boys are creating some kind of ruckus." With a glint in her eye, she says, "Your mom's property is perfect for his needs."

Before I can agree, Brooklyn runs over to me. "I'm going to go wait for my mom out front."

"Not without me, you're not." Before leaving, I turn back to Kelly. "Fine. I'll leave the key in the front office for him."

"You won't be sorry." She smiles endearingly.

I'm pretty sure she's wrong about that. I decide to charge Zachary Hart double the normal rate for the annoyance his presence is sure to cause me. Plus, a pain-in-the-butt tax of fifty percent. Let's see how he appreciates his peace and quiet now.

After safely delivering Brooklyn to her mother, I walk across the rink parking lot to my own car. I don't have any more lessons today, so I'll go home and let my mom know about her new tenant. I'm sure she'll be thrilled, even though I'm anything but.

My heart sinks as I climb into my sixteen-year-old Honda. Its interior is deplorable. Not only is it fading, but the seats were ripped by the previous owner's dog, and they've gotten worse since I've had it. No amount of duct tape or cheap seat covers can make it right.

Even though I'm grateful to have a mechanically reliable car, I'd really love to own something better looking. Unfortunately, all my spare cash goes to trying to keep my mom in her own home. A new car is about three thousandth on my list of things to purchase —currently smack between an on-demand hot water heater and a tropical vacation full of sandy beaches and fruity drinks sporting umbrellas.

After pulling out of the parking lot, I veer onto Maple Road—the tall evergreens and winding pavement not only relax me, but they help restore my equilibrium. The serenity of my surroundings quickly transforms my mood, and by the time I hit Maple Falls' downtown area, my red-hot anger toward Zachary Hart has been replaced by mild annoyance.

Driving by my old store front, I see that it's being turned into a frozen yogurt shop—which I predict will be a hit. I'm guessing people would rather eat froyo than buy a gorgeous bouquet to brighten their surroundings. Personally, I would want both.

Even though there aren't a lot of big business opportunities in my little town, I don't care. Maple Falls has everything I want. It's idyllically picturesque, the people are friendly, and it's home to my best childhood memories. Actually, all of my childhood memories, which makes me perfectly content to spend the rest of my life here.

Within minutes of turning left at Higgens Market, I pull into the driveway of my mom's house, and my current home. I gave up living on my own so I can be on hand whenever I'm needed. My biggest concern was Mom requiring help in the middle of the night, and my not being able to get to her fast enough.

Letting myself into the charming, if not slightly shabby sage-colored bungalow, I call out, "I'm home!"

My gaze passes through the living room toward the lift chair I recently picked up at the secondhand store. My mom is nearly standing when she sees me. Leaning forward onto the walker in front of her, she says, "You're early."

"I have some news."

I cringe as she makes the final push to her feet. I haven't seen her stand without assistance in more months than I care to remember. Looking up, she takes her first painful step. "I hope it's *good* news."

"Kelly found someone to rent out the cottage for two months."

"That *is* wonderful!" My mom takes another slow step.

Moving toward her, I ask, "Can I help you?"

She laughs, "Not unless you want to carry me."

She's lost so much weight this year, I probably could. "I think we should consider getting you a wheelchair."

She always pooh poohs the idea, so I'm surprised when she says, "Maybe after two months of rent coming in the door, we will."

"If you need one now, Mom, we should go ahead and get it." I hate that finances are keeping her from securing the aid she needs.

"I'm not ready yet." Then in her typically positive way, she adds, "I'm going to dance with the Rockettes before I sit down for good." My parents used to ballroom dance, and they loved nothing more than to waltz around together. I loved watching them.

"You're not joining the Rockettes without me," I tease.

My mom stops her haltingly slow progress across the room. "I'm not sure the cottage is even habitable. I haven't been out there in months."

"I'm heading out back now to see what needs to be done," I tell her. I'm guessing at this point in its vacancy, the list of chores will not only be extensive, but exhausting. Maybe I should charge His Royal Moneybags *three* times the rent.

"Let me know if you need any help. In the meantime, I'm going to take a little nap." My mom is only in her late fifties, but being in constant pain has made her look and act much older than her years.

What's really heartbreaking is there was a time she ran circles around everyone. She was active through my entire childhood. In addition to dancing, she participated in marathons, she biked, and she even started rock climbing. Then she turned fifty and was diagnosed with a progressive form of osteoarthritis. Now she can't even walk without assistance.

In the kitchen, I gather a bucket full of cleaning supplies before unlatching the back door and heading down the path that leads to the rental unit. It's still postcard-charming from a distance, but up close is another story. Not only has the paint started to peel, but the windows are so filthy you can hardly see through them. The shrubs are overgrown, and the flower bed is full of weeds. I could work out here for a month and still not bring it back to its former glory.

As I stick my key in the door, I say a small prayer that the inside won't be as bad. The hinges creak loudly, causing a chill to shoot up my spine. But instead of turning around and running for the hills, which is what I'd like to do, I reach in and flip on the light switch. Inhaling deeply, I cross the threshold. The sheets covering the furniture are dusty, but surprisingly everything else appears to be in decent shape. No raccoons nesting in the living room, no squirrels playing canasta at the kitchen table.

From where I'm standing, I can nearly see the whole cottage. There's a tiny kitchen, a snug living room—with fireplace—and a bedroom suite. In addition, there's a small back porch that over-looks Maple Creek, which is where I learned to swim as a little girl.

Pulling out my phone, I check the Wi-Fi signal. Luckily, I can still connect to the house. I press play on my deep-cleaning playlist and let the driving rhythms of old-time rock music put me in a good mood. I even manage to forget who I'm doing all this work for.

For the briefest moment, I consider that Kelly might be right about Zach. After all, he's Troy's brother, so how bad could the guy possibly be?

CHAPTER THREE

Zach

"Are you sure you don't want to come with me?" I ask Belle while filling my suitcase with casual clothes.

Sarcastic laughter is her only response.

"You'd love Washington state," I tell her. "It's green and gorgeous, and full of the best fish you've ever eaten."

She positions her fists aggressively on her hips, while demanding, "How do you know? Have you ever been there?"

Shrugging, I tell her, "I visited Seattle several years ago. But Troy loves it there." I stop what I'm doing and look over at her. Belle is average height and quite pretty—even though she dresses plainly and doesn't play up her looks in any way. She's incredibly organized and scathingly sharp-witted. When she interviewed for the job, she told me she didn't care how rich I was, she was never going to sleep with me, so I'd better get my mind out of the gutter. After assuring her my intentions were pure, she quickly became the best assistant I've ever had. She's also become something of a little sister—a *bossy* little sister.

Despite my praise for Maple Falls, Belle says, "I'm not going.

In fact, I'm looking forward to taking a break from you, and I can't do that in Washington."

"You still have to work while I'm gone," I remind her, cringing at the thought of what my life would be without her.

She cocks her brow dubiously. "Obviously. I mean, you're still going to be you, right? I'll just put out fires from afar. It'll probably be easier without you parading about town causing trouble."

"I don't *parade*."

"Not in the marching band kind of way," she assures me. "It's more of a royal strut."

"That's mean," I pout.

Belle pushes me to the side. "Just because I don't sugarcoat the truth doesn't mean I'm being nasty. Now get going and let me finish packing."

On my way out the door, I ask, "Is the plane ready to go?"

"Of course not," she laughs. "Didn't I tell you you're taking the bus?"

"I've been on my fair share of Greyhounds," I remind her.

"Yes, yes, I know." She rolls her eyes. "Back when you were poor. Go tell *People* magazine."

"Hey, I *was* poor once." I didn't start making real money until I got into crypto currency eight years ago. It turns out I'm something of a savant when it comes to the buying and selling of speculative currency.

Belle starts tucking rolled-up balls of socks into the corners of my suitcase. "Yes, Zach, I know. And while that's all very charming, I'm going to need you to go pack up your laptop." I feel like I've just been dismissed by my mother.

The limo driver calls up ten minutes later to tell me he's at the rear entrance of the building because the front is still covered with reporters. *What now?*

As Belle wheels my suitcase out of the bedroom, I ask her, "Why are reporters still stalking me? I thought things were slowing down."

"Yolanda gave an interview to *Hollywood Tonight* yesterday," she says.

"Were you planning on telling me?"

She shakes her head. "I was hoping I wouldn't have to."

My shoulders slump. "That bad?"

"The same as always."

"You mean she's telling everyone what a stingy lothario I am?"

Nodding her head sharply, Belle says, "I'll go down with you and put this in the trunk. If any reporters show up, you stay in the building, and I'll pretend I'm the one leaving."

"And then you'll go to Washington instead of me?" I joke.

Her blue eyes narrow perceptibly. "I'll drive around the block and we'll try it again."

Luckily, there's no press at the back exit and it looks like I'm going to make a clean getaway.

I tell Belle, "You might as well stay at my place while I'm gone. I mean, at least that way you won't have to deal with traffic." Belle lives in Pasadena and even though that's only twenty-five miles from my place, it still makes her commute well over an hour.

Instead of thanking me for the generous offer, she pushes me into the car. "Bye."

While buckling up, I wonder what kind of men my assistant likes. More importantly, I wonder what kind of guy would put up with her. I can't imagine she's all that popular a date with that blunt demeanor of hers.

Luckily, the drive to the Santa Monica airport only takes thirty minutes, and I use the time to make a dent in my inbox. Twenty minutes after boarding I'm in the air and on my way to what I hope is going to be a trip that not only ends my bad press, but will be a nice break from all the chaos in my life. I'm not delusional enough to think it will be a real vacation, but it's got to be better than suffering through the maelstrom of a PR nightmare.

I told my brother I was going to arrive on Friday, but I'm coming a day early so that if he slips up and tells anyone, I can avoid any trouble at the airport. I'd like to get a lay of the land before everyone knows I'm there.

Opening my laptop, I spot an email from Yolanda. It reads:

Zach,

You know by now that you've messed with the wrong girl. If you would like me to quit my campaign you need to call me. I have a proposition.

Yolanda

My first reaction is one of frustration. Even though the subtext of Yolanda's note suggests extortion, she doesn't come right out and say what her proposal is. So, it's possible no one else would interpret her email as menacingly as I have. So much for using it to show the world what her real intentions are—which, as far as I'm concerned, is more attention for herself.

Even though I'm sorely tempted to call her and find out what she wants, I don't want to give her the pleasure of knowing she's causing me trouble. Like the government, I have a longstanding policy of not negotiating with terrorists, and I will not succumb to Yolanda's guerrilla tactics—even if it means getting my life back on track.

Once my plane lands, I grab my bags and hightail it across the tarmac to the SUV Belle arranged to have waiting. I know the black Trailblazer is for me because it's the only automobile on site. Peeking in the window, I spot another giveaway—the key fob is sitting on the middle console.

After stowing my luggage in the back hatch, I climb into the driver's seat. Kelly told me to pick up the key to my lodgings at the rink, so I program the address into Waze. Then I sit back and enjoy a traffic-free drive through what I can honestly call paradise.

I steer my way around a winding road that traverses a heavily wooded landscape. I wouldn't exactly call the thoroughfare a highway as I only pass four cars and I have to stop to let two deer cross the road. What a strange dichotomy between traffic here and traffic in LA.

When the map app tells me my destination is only five hundred feet away, I start to get excited. I barely see the break in the trees until I'm on top of my turn. That's when the landscape opens to a parking lot. The skating arena isn't far away.

After pulling into a space close to the front entrance, I get out of the car and take a deep breath. The air still smells like summer, but the cooler temperature hints that autumn has arrived. Even though the weather eventually cools in Southern California, the mercury often stays well over a hundred degrees into October which, plainly put, is miserable.

I pass four little girls and their mothers as I walk inside the building, and no one takes notice of me. No double takes, no curious gazes—it's like I've landed in a world where I'm nothing special, and I couldn't be happier about that.

Inside the lobby, I look around for the office. When I spot it, I head in that direction only to discover the door is locked. Pulling out my phone from my pocket, I reread the text from Kelly.

KELLY

The key to your cabin will be waiting for you in the office. Give us a call once you're settled.

Turning around, I walk into the stands surrounding the rink and look for someone who might possess access to the locked room. The only people I see are an instructor and a small class of pint-sized skaters. There are some parents sitting and watching, but no one looks official. As such, I decide to sit down and wait for the lesson to be over.

The young woman teaching the class tells her group, "No jumps today. We're going to work on making your turns more graceful. Figure skaters should look like angels gliding through the clouds."

Even from this distance I can see the teacher is quite lovely. Her dark hair is pulled back, making the sharp angles of her cheek bones stand out. Yet, it's the pink fullness of her lips that really grabs my attention. She's wearing yoga pants and a form-fitting long-sleeve top which leaves little to the imagination. This woman is taller and curvier than your average figure skater. She's also a total knock-out.

I remind myself that I am not here in pursuit of women. In fact, the opposite is true. I'm here to avoid romantic entanglements and halt the demise of my lagging reputation, both courtesy of Yolanda Simms. I make a mental note not to forget that.

A red-headed girl raises her hand, and says, "Miss Ellie, I have to tinkle."

Ellie—I like that name—turns her head slightly while pointing to the exit. "Hurry up, Taylor. And make sure to take your skates off."

"But that'll take forever!" the little girl moans.

Ellie shakes her head. "Which is why you're all supposed to use the bathroom before we start." Then she addresses the class. "Who wants to show everyone what it looks like to be a graceful figure skater?"

Another little girl raises her hand. This one appears to be slightly older than the others, maybe ten or eleven. "I'll do it, Miss Ellie," she says before standing and removing her skate guards.

The teacher leads the way to the center of the rink, gliding in an elongated figure-eight. "Follow me, Claire."

Once Ellie completes her final rotation she leans forward and raises one leg, stretching her arms out to her sides as she glides forth. I've never thought of figure skating as an erotic sport until this moment. The instructor looks more like a pin-up girl than an athlete, and I'm finding it difficult to watch her and still maintain an aura of indifference.

"Zach!" I turn to see my brother Troy approaching. "You're early." His smile stretches across his face, leaving little doubt how happy he is that I'm there.

"I couldn't wait to see you," I fib. I haven't seen Troy in almost a year, and even though I really do miss him, I wouldn't be here at all if my life wasn't in the toilet.

Reaching out, he pulls me into his arms for a bear hug. "Liar. You wanted to get here ahead of the press."

"Guilty," I confess before adding, "The office is locked, so I couldn't get the key to the cabin Kelly found for me."

Stepping back, Troy tells me, "I don't have it yet. We can wait for Ellie's class to end and get it from her."

My face flushes with heat. "I'm staying with the figure skating instructor?" No good can possibly come from that if my goal is to save my reputation.

Troy knocks his fist into my shoulder. "Dream on, buddy. You're not staying *with* Ellie. Your cottage is at the back of her mom's property."

I feel the need to confirm, "So, she lives somewhere else?"

Troy's eyebrows knit closer together before he clarifies, "Ellie lives with her mom. Elaine is in bad health and needs assistance."

"So, she'll be close to me?" Beads of sweat pop up on my forehead. *What in the world is wrong with me?* I'm acting like a kid in the throes of puberty.

"Is that a problem?"

Changing the direction of the conversation, I tell my brother, "I'm excited to take a break from my crazy life."

That's when Ellie turns around and spots us. Her eyes narrow and her body visibly tenses. Is it me or does she look like she's preparing to go to war? "Are you sure she's okay with me staying at her cottage?" I ask Troy. "She looks like she wants to bludgeon me with her skate blade."

Troy laughs heartily. "You aren't supposed to be here until

tomorrow and according to Kelly, Ellie has been busting her butt to get the cottage ready for you. I don't think she's done yet."

"I'm fine with whatever shape it's in," I tell him. And even though that's true, I can't help but hope Ellie isn't as prickly as she looks.

CHAPTER FOUR

Ellie

Of course, Zachary Hart showed up early. The man is clearly so self-absorbed he thinks the world's population is here for no other reason than to serve him. I turn toward my class and announce, "Everyone on the ice. Practice your revolutions until I come back." Then I skate toward the opening in the boards where Troy is standing next to his brother.

"Hey, Ellie," Troy greets. "How's it going? The kids look like they're having a blast."

"Thanks to you and Kelly," I tell him. "These girls wouldn't be skating without you."

Troy passes off the compliment in that aw-shucks self-depre-cating manner of his. "Sure they would. They'd just have to wait until the ponds froze up in the winter." He reaches an arm out toward his brother. "Zach came a day early. I hope that won't be a problem." Before I can answer, he adds, "Zach, this is Ellie Butler."

I shift my attention in the billionaire's direction, with every intention of giving him a piece of my mind. But as soon as our eyes meet, my throat constricts, making coherent verbal communication impossible—on my part anyway.

Zach is way hotter than he looks in the tabloids and on TV. He also possesses a magnetic aura that's drawing me in—like I inexplicably want to jump into his arms. *How is that even possible since I fervently loathe him?*

Mr. Smug extends his hand to shake mine. "I wanted to get here ahead of the press."

My eyes drop to the offered hand and bounce back to stare at his—dang it—handsome face. Keeping both of my arms at my sides, I tell him, "The cottage won't be ready until tomorrow."

"I was worried it wouldn't," Troy says. "But that's no problem. Zach can stay with us for the night. The boys can't wait to see him."

Zach has other ideas. "I don't mind if it isn't perfect." He continues, "I'm going to need a quiet place to work, and my nephews are anything but quiet."

"Then you should stay at the lodge," I tell him, unwilling to budge on his occupation date.

"That won't work for me."

"Why?" I demand incredulously. *Does this guy really think the entire world is at his beck and call?*

"Because the team arrives tomorrow, and the press will be on site. I don't want to be anywhere near them until I'm ready."

I unconsciously look at his fingernails and wonder if he gets manicures. Sure enough, there are no cuticles, and his nails look shiny and buffed.

"Afraid they'll make you look bad?" My sarcasm is heavy.

Zach's shoulders square off like he's turned to stone. "Excuse me?" He's clearly not used to anyone standing up to him.

"The cottage will be ready tomorrow after three," I tell him firmly. "The key will be waiting for you in the office." I glance at Troy to make sure I haven't made him angry, but he looks nothing short of amused.

"I need to stay there *tonight*," Zach says more firmly than he should for a man with no control over the situation.

"Good luck with that." I know I'm taking things too far, but I can't seem to stop myself.

Richie Rich runs a hand through his hair like he's going to rip it out. "Ellie, is it?" He knows darn well that's my name, so I don't respond. "What is it going to take for me to get into your mother's cottage right now?"

I motion toward my class before telling him, "A genie in a lamp. You got one of those?" I don't wait for him to answer. "I'm in class right now, and there's no way I can leave the rink for at least another forty minutes."

Troy's phone rings but he doesn't bother to answer it. Instead, without even looking down, he pushes the button to send the call to voicemail. His gaze continues to bounce between me and his brother, obviously enjoying our heated exchange.

"I can wait forty minutes," Zach says.

"*Or*, you could wait until tomorrow after three." There's no way he can expect to check into a hotel early. Although maybe *he* would.

"Ellie." Zach inhales deeply before slowly releasing the pent-up breath. "I need to get settled in the cottage today, and I need you to tell me what you require to make that happen."

This guy isn't going to give it a rest, so I say the most ridiculous thing that comes to mind. "You'll need to roll up your sleeves and help me finish cleaning it." A man like him would never go for that in a million years.

Before I can celebrate my win, he says, "Fine. I'll wait for your class to end and then you can take me to my new home."

What? "I'm putting you in charge of all the windows, inside and out," I threaten. He's sure to back off now.

"No problem."

I suddenly feel like I'm living a fever dream. "Cleaning windows in the woods is a dirty job. It takes a lot of time and elbow grease."

"I know what cleaning windows means." He stares down at me like he's my overlord and I'm an insignificant serf.

Well, two can play that game, mister. "You have to get my stamp of approval and I'm not going to let you leave any streaks," I warn.

Troy tries to cover his laughter with a cough but he's not successful. I'm glad someone is having a good time.

"Ellie," Zach says calmly, "go finish your class. I'll be waiting here when you're done."

We're at a standstill. I don't know how I'm going to get away from this situation. I obviously cannot finish my class because he just now told me to. The only thing I can do now is plot to make Zach's afternoon of cleaning as miserable as possible. While that sounds like a lot of fun, spending any time near him is sure to be a chore. I'm furious with myself for my reaction—my hands are sweaty, and my heart is pounding like a teenager in love. Being that I'm neither a teenager nor in love, I should be stone-cold indifferent to Zachary Hart.

Troy interrupts my thoughts. "You two should place a wager."

"On how well I clean windows?" Zach seems appalled by the idea, which makes me a real fan of it.

"If you don't clean them to my satisfaction, you'll have to pay an extra month's rent," I decide.

"And if I clean them to your standards, I get a free month's rent?"

"Hardly," I snap. "If you clean them to my standards then you get to stay there tonight." I'm going to lose even more respect for Zach if he doesn't tell me what to do with this bet before storming away.

"Fine." Zach turns around and sits down on the bleachers. He pulls his phone out of his pocket and starts tapping away. I've been dismissed.

"Soooo," Troy says. "It looks like you've got everything under control here ..."

"Please tell Kelly I'll be over tomorrow morning," I tell Troy before turning around and skating back to my class. Who does Zachary Hart think he is? How dare he force himself into his lease ahead of schedule? And more importantly, why is he so eager to wash windows?

For the next forty minutes, I valiantly try to focus on my aspiring figure skaters. I'm only half successful as my gaze is repeatedly drawn to the bleachers where Zach is sitting. He's so engrossed in his telephone, he doesn't look at me once. Which makes me even madder.

For obvious reasons, I'm reluctant to end the lesson, so I keep the kids on the ice until their parents start to come up to get them. I'd keep teaching until midnight if I could, but that doesn't appear to be an option. There's a three-day weekend coming up and everyone is trying to get in their last camping adventure of the year. From what I hear, folks have already started setting up their tents by the river.

Once all the kids are off the ice, I sit down on the bench to take off my skates. I wonder if I could feign illness to get out of spending the afternoon with Zachary Hart. Yet the man is so pigheaded he'd probably agree to clean the whole cabin himself.

I'm so engrossed in my task, I don't realize I've been snuck up on until I hear, "You ready to go?"

I don't have to look up to know who's doing the asking. I simply hiss, "Yessss." Then I grab my skates and turn toward the exit. In a slow march, I lead the way like I'm heading to my own execution.

CHAPTER FIVE

Zach

I don't expect everyone to like me, but Ellie Butler has taken things to a new level. She has the disposition of a startled rattlesnake. In a bid to engage her in safe conversation, I ask, "Have you worked at the rink for long?"

She steps down into the parking lot before answering. "No."

I try again. "Were you a professional skater at one time?" *Come on, lady, give me something.*

Ellie scoffs loudly. "Hardly."

"Why hardly? You seemed pretty good out there to me." Her elegantly graceful lines made it impossible for me to look away.

She stops walking, causing me to nearly run her over. Stepping back to widen the space between us, she demands, "How many professional figure skaters do you know who are five ten?"

I shrug my shoulders. "None. But I don't know any professional figure skaters."

"Maria Sotskova was five eight and that was considered shocking."

"And she is ..."

Ellie rolls her eyes before demanding, "Do you know anything about ice sports?"

"I was a winger on my college hockey team," I tell her. "I was top pick for the draft my senior year before a knee injury benched me for good."

"Oh." *Is it me or does she look annoyed by my answer?*

Trying for a safer topic, I ask, "How long have you lived in Maple Falls?"

"My whole life."

"I grew up in Michigan," I tell her. Even though she doesn't give any indication she cares, I add, "Grand Rapids."

Silence. I stop walking at my SUV. "Do you want me to drive you to your car?"

She keeps moving. "No." Then she points ahead of her. "I'm just over there."

Getting into my ride, I follow closely behind her. I have a feeling Ellie might try to lose me if I'm not fast enough. She stops at a generic-looking sedan and gets in. It takes her nearly five minutes before she backs out.

Once we're on our way, I let my mind wander. I can't imagine what it would be like to have only lived in one place my whole life. While I liked Grand Rapids well enough, I didn't let the door hit me in the backside when I left town. I was ready to see the world the minute I graduated from high school.

I moved to Southern California right after college and quickly became absorbed in the culture, which is like nowhere else in the world. Somehow living in LA makes you feel entitled to beautiful days and beautiful people. It's a place where looks matter and where you dine is considered a near religious pilgrimage. Don't get me wrong, I've enjoyed my time there, but I've recently started feeling it's losing its luster.

Regardless of my earlier concern that Ellie would try to leave me behind, she drives slowly. Like below the speed limit. I follow her through an inviting downtown area that boasts signs for a farmers' market and an upcoming Maple Festival. The more I see, the more charmed I am by Maple Falls.

Ellie turns left at what appears to be the only grocery store in town. A short way later, she turns right into a driveway leading to an older-looking green house. She motions for me to park next to her in front of a double garage.

Getting out of my SUV, I ask, "Is this the cottage I'm renting?"

Her face scrunches up in disbelief. "No. This is where I live with my mom. Your place isn't even close to this nice." She takes off down a cobble stone path that leads behind the house toward a wood chip trail that's been overtaken by weeds.

I don't see the cottage right away which makes me wonder if Ellie isn't leading me on a wild goose chase—like Hansel and Gretel being taken deep into the woods by their father.

"Are you sure you know where you're going?" I call out.

She ignores me and keeps walking. When I finally see the bungalow, I realize that while not impressive, it appears sound enough. The biggest boon is that it's in the middle of nowhere. There will be no media circus surrounding me here, primarily because no one could ever find it.

Stopping at the front door, my landlady declares, "Look at the filth on these windows. Still think you're up for the job?"

I shrug my shoulders. "They don't look so bad."

She sticks a key into the front door and opens it. "Oh, they're bad. You should see the ones in the back."

A sense of déjà vu hits me hard as I step into the small house. I can count on one hand the times I've felt this kind of familiarity being somewhere I know I've never been in my conscious life.

Ellie crosses her arms in a belligerent fashion and demands, "Not fancy enough for you?"

"Not at all. It's very nice." That's a bit of an overstatement, but I'm not going to explain my sixth sense reaction. Most people don't buy into that kind of stuff.

Walking into the kitchen, Ellie announces, "I was going to go to the market today to buy you some of the basics, but now that you're here you can do that for yourself." She pulls out a bucket and puts it in the sink before squirting soap into it. "It'll be easier for you to wash the windows down first before using window cleaner on them."

"My mom used to do that too," I tell her. *Could we be on the verge of bonding over household chores?*

"Have you washed any windows since you were a kid?" She's back to sounding like I'm an incompetent annoyance.

"I don't think so. Most guys aren't great housekeepers."

Ellie opens the cabinet beneath the sink and removes a big sponge. Submerging it in the bucket, she disparagingly says, "You probably hire someone to do it for you."

"Is there something wrong with hiring people to do things you'd rather not do?"

She turns her back toward me and tends to the bucket. "I suppose not if you can afford it."

Finally, a hint as to why she dislikes me. "You don't like rich people," I decide.

"I like your brother and Kelly just fine." She doesn't elaborate beyond that. While Troy and Kelly do well for themselves, they are nowhere near my tax bracket, but somehow, I don't think Ellie would appreciate hearing that.

"Then it's just me you don't like."

Ellie hefts the bucket out of the sink and drops it onto the floor with a thud. "I don't know you."

"And yet you are supremely irritated by my existence."

Drying her hands on a dishtowel, she says, "I have a busy schedule, Mr. Hart. I don't like people interfering with it."

I drop my briefcase onto the table. "You'd think I was making your life easier by helping clean."

Her expression takes a trip through several emotions—frustration, hostility, disbelief— before finally settling on indifference. "They're not clean yet."

"Would you mind if I changed clothes first?" I ask. Pointing to my sweater, I add, "Cashmere doesn't like water."

She looks predictably exasperated. "Do whatever you want." Then she opens a cabinet and starts to pull out other cleaning products. "I'll get to work in here."

I turn around and give myself a quick tour of my rental. I imagine I'll have a fire burning whenever I'm here, so I call out, "Is there firewood on the property or do I need to bring that in?"

I hear her disembodied voice from the other room. "Mom and I get a cord every season for our wood-burning stove. There's plenty, but you'll need to come up to the house and bring it down yourself." Is it me or is there a hint of challenge in her tone? Like now she thinks I'm incapable of carrying wood.

The bedroom is tiny and hosts nothing more than a full-size bed and chest of drawers. Instead of breaking into my suitcase, I decide to simply pull off my sweater and work in my t-shirt.

Ellie is already scrubbing the kitchen floor when I come out, so I don't bother her. I just grab the bucket she prepared and carry it out the front door. Washington in the fall is beautiful. The sun is shining, and while there are a few clouds in the sky, they're not rain clouds. They're more like the cotton candy variety I'm used to from my childhood.

Standing on the small porch, I look out toward the woods and notice a hammock hanging between two large maple trees. I haven't lain in one of those since I was a kid. I'm suddenly tempted to postpone getting to work in favor of taking a quick lie down. Then I think of how Ellie would react if she caught me slacking off and decide to get to work.

Bending over, I pull the sponge out of the bucket and soap the window next to the front door. There's something almost hypnotic about watching the circular motion of my hand, and I quickly become lost in my thoughts.

The biggest one being, how can I make Ellie like me? Despite her surly disposition, I'm more than a little intrigued by her.

CHAPTER SIX

Ellie

I have to repeatedly tell myself to stop staring at my mom's new tenant. Zach took off his sweater and is washing the glass in his t-shirt—an item of clothing so fitted I can count his six-pack. Make that a twelve-pack. *Why in the world did I say he could move in today if he helped clean?*

Yet, even as I ask that question, I know the answer. I couldn't say no with Troy standing right next to me. He and Kelly have been so good to me that I felt like I had no choice but to let his brother move in today.

Hurrying to take the curtains off the rods, I remind myself that Zach Hart is nothing but an entitled, self-absorbed, womanizing cheapskate. I'm relieved when my phone rings as I am on the way to the window where Zach is working. Turning around, I sit down at the kitchen table with my back to him.

"Hello?"

"Hey, it's Kiki." My childhood friend, Keira, sounds panicked. "I just heard the most awful rumor."

"What's that?"

"That Dan Roberts is coming back to town to do that charity team Troy Hart is setting up."

"Ah, your high school sweetheart. The one that got away," I tease.

"The very same." She sounds despondent. Poor Kiki. Sometimes I think if she channeled her focus from Dan onto anything else—say, learning a foreign language—she would probably be speaking six different ones by now. Fluently. "I figured you might have heard something from Troy at the arena."

"Dan may have gotten away *then*, but there's no telling what might happen with him coming back to town."

A low growl emanates from the receiver. "I'm not going to make a play for Dan. He's a gorgeous, famous, amazing hockey player living the high life in Chicago. I'm just a boring hometown girl who runs the local farmers' market. Yawn." Before I can tell her how wonderful she is, she adds, "And besides, there wouldn't be any future in it. It's not like Dan is planning to stick around Maple Falls. He'll be here for the games and then he'll be gone."

"*You* are gorgeous and amazing, Kiki," I tell my friend. She has never had the self-confidence she should. She's got no idea how beautiful she really is. And smart. "Don't you dare let any man make you feel like you're less than that. Also, you have no idea where Dan is going to end up."

"Uh-huh." She's clearly placating me because she changes the subject. "What are you up to?"

"I'm cleaning the cottage out back. We've rented it to one of Troy's brothers for a couple months."

"Which brother?" She sounds intrigued.

"Zach." I nearly spit his name.

She starts laughing. "The hottie billionaire? Poor you!"

"I loathe him," I remind her.

"I think the lady doth protest too much."

"Are you quoting Shakespeare at me or something?" I ask my bookish friend. Kiki was the nerd in the jock-nerd couple of her and Dan back in high school.

"All I'm saying is that the guy's a smoke show."

"I have to go," I tell her. "The hottie billionaire, as you call him, is outside washing the windows and he missed a spot."

"Wait, what?!"

"I'll fill you in later." I put my phone down and stride out the front door—something I regret doing as soon as I walk around to the side of the house. Zach is standing there in a very wet T-shirt. It's so clingy he might as well not be wearing anything at all. My mouth responds by going as dry as the Sahara.

Zach looks up at me and stops scrubbing the window. "Can I help you?" He sounds vaguely angry, which I like. I'd hate to think he was out here enjoying himself.

I nearly tell him to put his sweater back on, but suddenly I can't seem to talk. The only sound I'm capable of is, "Gah …"

"Excuse me?" He looks concerned.

"Grrrr …" I utter while praying a bolt of lightning will zap through the sky and strike me down.

Zach puts his sponge back into the bucket before walking toward me. "Are you okay?" His caring tone is nearly my undoing.

"Um … yeah … agggg …"

As soon as he's in front of me, he reaches over and touches the side of my mouth to wipe away a trickle of moisture. So much for dry mouth, I'm positively drooling over the guy. The only way to regain my dignity is to succumb to a major cardiac event. Unsure how to go about that, I roll my eyes skyward in a desperate bid the Almighty will take pity on me.

Zach suddenly reaches out and grabs my arms. "Are you having a seizure?"

I only see two options for myself. I could probably come up with more if the blood could get to my brain and allow me to think, but it can't seem to make the journey.

The first thing I can do is to tell Zach my body is betraying my common sense and that I think he's a hunka hunka burning love. Luckily, a tiny voice inside my brain stops me from doing this.

That's why I go with the second option—which is to fake a faint and hope Zach catches me before I hit the ground and hurt myself for real. Being that his hands are already on my arms, I'm hoping his reflexes will be up to the task.

On a wing and a prayer, I collapse with the grace of a lead balloon in triple gravity. Zach's arms wrap around me fiercely and I nearly swoon for real as he pulls me close to his heart. "Ellie, I'm here. I have you."

I want to yell at him to let me go, but as I'm mid pretend swoon, I can't. Zach picks me up—in his arms!—and carries me inside the cottage. I crack my eyelids a fraction to see where he's taking me only to hear him say, "Oh, good, you're awake!" He takes me to the sofa but instead of putting me down, he sits with me still on his lap. It's pure torture.

"You can put me down," I croak.

He doesn't. Instead, he demands, "Are you okay? Should I take you to the hospital?"

The thought of showing up at Maple Falls Memorial fills me with dread and I shiver in response. I cannot afford to fake a stroke. My health insurance deductible is so high I'd have to really be dying to make it worth the amount of money I'd have to fork over for whatever tests they'd run.

Inhaling deeply, I tell him, "I'm good. I just haven't eaten today." I don't mention the three-egg omelet with toast and hash browns I consumed at the diner only three hours ago. Oh, and that piece of blackberry pie. A la mode.

"Is there *anything* in the kitchen?" he wants to know. "An energy bar, nuts, a stick of jerky?"

I shake my head while inadvertently inhaling his spicy scent—the clove and orange scent makes me dizzy for real. "I told you I haven't gotten to the market yet."

He stands up with me still in his arms and declares, "I'll take you up to your house then. We can get you something there."

There is no way my mom can see me carried into our house by Zachary Hart. No. Way. "I'm fine, thank you. Just put me down."

"I can't do that. Either I take you up to your house or I take you out for lunch. You decide."

Squirming in his arms, I tell him, "That's not necessary, Zach. Please put me down."

His response is to squeeze tighter.

It appears I have no recourse. "Fine, you can take me to the market, and I'll buy something for lunch."

Walking toward the door, he announces, "We passed a diner on the way here. I'm taking you there first."

I say a small prayer that Shirley May is not pulling a double today. She'd out me for sure if she saw me again so soon. It's not that I care if Zach thinks I'm a liar. It's just that I really need to have the moral high ground here.

Between the two of us, I'm not the bad guy.

CHAPTER SEVEN

Zach

I should not be having feelings for my feisty landlady, except she's in my arms and boy howdy, it feels right. I forcefully remind myself I'm in Maple Falls to stay out of trouble. I'm not here to make my problems worse.

I don't say anything to Ellie as I carry her up the path to my SUV. Primarily because I'm sure I'd say something wildly inappropriate. Like, you're gorgeous; I love the feel of your soft curves; and what do you say we get married tonight?

When we arrive at my rental car—three hours later, or so it seems—I gently put Ellie down so that she's leaning against the fender. Then I take out my keys and open the passenger side for her.

Once she's inside, I close the door and hurry around to the driver's side. Getting in, I announce, "I could use a big fat cheeseburger right about now. How about you?"

She hems and haws for a minute before answering, "I'm not really hungry."

"That's too bad because you're eating." I know I sound dictatorial, but I'm over women who refuse to feed their bodies the calories needed for basic human function. And if Ellie hasn't eaten yet today, she must be starving.

"You can't tell me what to do," she says with hostility.

"You fainted from hunger," I remind her. "You're going to eat."

She stays quiet until we're on the main drag where the diner is located. "I thought you had things to do today."

"I do." With a sly grin, I add, "I have windows to wash."

"Ha, ha. I thought you had important businessman things to do which is why you couldn't stay with your brother."

The main reason I didn't want to stay at Troy's is because I was enjoying giving Ellie a hard time. She didn't hide her dislike for me very well, and I seem to have taken that as a challenge. "I can work after we eat and after the windows are done."

She grumbles but remains quiet until I park in front of the diner. That's when she tries again. "I really am okay with grabbing an energy bar at the market."

Instead of responding, I turn off the ignition and step out of the car. I run around to let her out, but she's already exited on her own. Taking her arm, I warn, "Be careful. You don't want to expend a lot of energy before we get you refueled."

A few steps later, I open the front door to the typical small-town diner. The décor is not trendy. Old school brown booths surround the perimeter of a room full of wooden chairs and tables that have probably been there for thirty years. It's nothing like eating out in Beverly Hills, and I love it on sight.

As soon as Ellie walks inside, her eyes immediately dart back and forth like she's looking for someone. A middle-aged woman in a pink dress raises her hand and greets, "You're back!"

Ellie's posture straightens like she just had a ramrod surgically implanted. "Shirley May!" She rushes toward the server and whispers something I can't hear.

I do, however, hear Shirley May's response. "Don't worry, hon. I won't say a thing." She winks at me and adds, "A little mystery is the key to any good relationship, am I right?" Ellie's complexion turns hot pink—ostensibly by the implication that we're an item.

Shirley May leads us to a booth in front of the window. Putting the laminated menus on the table, she announces, "It always slows down after the lunch rush. If you'd come two hours earlier, you'd probably have had to sit at the counter." Then she walks away.

As soon as Ellie and I are settled across from each other, I ask, "You come here often?"

I wouldn't have thought it possible, but her cheeks go even pinker than before. "It's the best breakfast and lunch in town."

"Better than the restaurant at Hawk River?" From the way Troy talks about his restaurant you'd think the chef had received a Michelin star or twelve.

Ellie looks up from her menu. "I don't eat at the lodge very often."

"That bad, huh?"

Her head drops to the side, and she glares at me like she's inspecting a particularly gnarly insect under a microscope. "It's expensive. Not everyone can eat out and not worry about the cost." And just like that, she's mad at me again.

"Ah." I don't know what else to say. Picking up my menu, I ask, "What's the best thing you've had here?"

"I like everything but the Monte Cristo, but that's only because I don't like sweet mixed with savory."

"I'm with you," I tell her. "My mom thinks a marshmallow crust on mashed sweet potatoes is gourmet fare. I've never been able to appreciate the combination."

"Do your parents still live in Michigan?"

"They sure do. As much as we've all tried to get them to move out west, they're still in the house we grew up in."

She seems surprised to hear this. "You'd think with such successful sons, you'd want to *improve* their lifestyle." She makes it sound like my folks moving closer to their sons wouldn't be any improvement at all.

"We've made sure to upgrade everything for them," I tell her. "Troy paid for new siding and a new roof, my twin Mac bought them a hot tub, and Jeffrey and Jacob built a guest house at the back of the property that my mom uses as an art studio."

"What did you do?" she demands none too nicely.

She clearly doesn't think I've done anything, so I particularly enjoy telling her, "I bought them a house in Barbados so they can escape the brutal winters." *Take that.*

"Oh."

After the waitress fills our water glasses and writes down our orders—I get the cheeseburger and Ellie gets a bowl of soup with half a sandwich—I say, "You don't seem to think highly of me. Why is that?"

Ellie squirms slightly in her seat. "Most people don't think much of you, do they?"

Until recently, I've been regarded as a pillar of society, or so I thought. I stare at her intently while taking a sip of my water. Then I put down the glass. "You're talking about my recent press."

When she nods her head, I ask, "Do you believe everything you hear?"

"Of course not."

"But you believe everything being said about me."

My lunch date suddenly looks uncomfortable. "Why would Yolanda Simms lie?"

"So, you're upset about Yolanda and not the earlier allegations that I don't give enough money to charity?"

"Neither puts you in a good light."

I nod my head slowly. "When you get to where I am in life, Ellie, you discover there are people who love nothing more than to tear you down."

"And where are you, Zach?" she sneers. "Far away from all the poor ordinary folks who make the world go 'round?"

This woman has got a chip on her shoulder the size of which I cannot fathom. What did I ever do to her but rent her cottage, wash her windows, and take her to lunch? "I think you've gotten the wrong impression of me."

"How's that?" she demands.

"You've jumped to conclusions, even though you obviously know very little about me."

Our waitress drops a basket of crackers on the table for Ellie's soup. Instead of answering my question, she pulls out a package and opens it. After eating two, she says, "It's true I don't know much about you, but I'd think if you were the good guy you want people to think you are, the press would have gotten wind of that."

There's no use fighting her. If she's got her mind set on my being a villain, so be it. It's probably even for the best, given the attraction I feel for her. I'm determined to leave Maple Falls as single as I was when I arrived, so I simply tell her, "I'm sure you're right." She seems surprised I'm not defending myself.

My cell phone rings as soon as our food arrives. "Belle, how are things at home?" I greet. "Did the plumber check the primary bathroom drain?" Without bothering to excuse myself, I push out of the booth and head to the front door so I can speak with my assistant in private.

"You've got bigger problems than a drain," Belle says. "I just got wind that Yolanda knows about your brother's charity hockey games. She's going to be in Maple Falls covering them for KBIZ." Without so much as a breath, she continues, "So much for your going up to Washington to reclaim your reputation."

My stomach rolls over like I just got off Space Mountain jacked up to twice the normal speed. In a bid to sound unbothered, I say, "She won't be the only reporter here."

"No, but that woman will do everything she can to poison the pool against you."

"This isn't my first rodeo. Let her do her worst."

"Uh-huh." Belle isn't buying my bravado. "I suggest you enjoy every minute before she gets there."

"You don't happen to know when that will be, do you?" Maybe I should just abandon ship and go back to LA.

"No idea. But I'll let you know when I find out."

Shaking my head I demand, "What in the world did I ever do to that woman?"

"You can't be serious?" Belle asks. Before I can assure her I am, she clarifies, "You spurned her in front of the whole world."

"I only said that we weren't an exclusive couple. Which, I assure you, we never were."

My assistant makes a low tsking sound. "You don't know much about women, do you, Zach?"

I think about how Ellie has been treating me for the last few hours before answering, "I guess I don't."

"Then you'd better do some studying," Belle says. "Because as soon as Yolanda shows up in Maple Falls, heads are going to roll. Starting with yours."

CHAPTER EIGHT

Ellie

Even though I don't approve of Zach's reputation, he's never been unkind to me. I mean, heck, he's washing the cottage windows and he's taking me to lunch. Having said that, I remind myself not to be sweet-talked into thinking he's anything more than he is—a man with more money than sense.

Zach comes back to the table a few minutes after leaving. He doesn't bother to say anything, he simply sits down and takes a bite of his cheeseburger. We eat in silence until Shirley May comes over with the check.

As she gives it to Zach, I tell him, "I'll pay for my own."

Pulling out a hundred-dollar bill from his billfold, he hands it to Shirley. "The bill is mine," he tells me with a smile. Then he turns back to Shirley May. "The change is yours."

She grabs the money and quite literally runs away with it. "That's a pretty big tip," I tell him.

He shrugs. "I like to leave a good tip when the service is good."

"Yeah, but you probably left her twice what the actual bill was." Why am I fighting him on this?

"What's your point?"

I wipe my mouth with my napkin before declaring, "You can't possibly do that every time you eat out."

His green eyes narrow slightly. "Why is that?"

My super articulate response is, "Because, well … you just can't."

Zach stands up. "Are you ready to head back to your house now or do you mind if we stop so I can get some groceries on the way?"

Getting out of the booth, I tell him, "We can stop. I need to pick up my mom's pain medication. The pharmacy is right next door to the market."

"I hope she's okay," he says while leading the way out to the car.

"She's got osteoarthritis," I tell him. "She's in a lot of pain."

Opening the car door for me, he asks, "Do you have her on a turmeric supplement? It's great for inflammation."

"I don't," I tell him. "Her doctor never mentioned that."

"Most western medicine practitioners push prescriptions, not natural remedies." Once he gets inside, he adds, "I think both have their place."

"Do you take turmeric?"

"Ever since my injury in college," he tells me. "I don't like the fuzzy-headedness I get from pain meds."

This is the last conversation I thought I'd be having with Zachary Hart. "Maybe I'll look for it at the pharmacy."

"I'll give you some when we get back to the cottage. That way your mom can try it for a couple of weeks to see if it works for her."

If I were in the mood to think nice things about Zach, I might think he was trying to save me money. Either way, it makes a small dent in my irritation toward him. "That would be nice, thank you."

Zach takes the first right turn and circles around the block until we're at the store. Once again, he walks around the car to open the door for me. This time I let him. "I'll meet you in the market after you're done at the pharmacy," he says before striding away.

I stand still and watch him, wondering what kind of man he really is. He's been decent to me, but he might be a different animal entirely with a woman he's romantically interested in.

I ponder that while I stroll over to the pharmacy. "Hey, Jamie. How are you?" I spot Jamie Feinberg, who was in my graduating class in high school. She left town to get her college degree and then came back and went into business with her dad as co-owner of the pharmacy. She's married to Mitch Hanks, another of our classmates, as well as being the town veterinarian.

"Ellie, how are you? How's your mom?"

"She's in a lot of pain. I'm here for her prescription."

Jamie turns around and looks through the filing cabinet until she finds my mom's medicine. "There's a twenty-dollar co-pay," she tells me.

While twenty bucks isn't a lot to ease my mom's discomfort, these things add up. "That's twice what it was last month," I tell her.

"The cost of everything is skyrocketing," she commiserates. "Do you know my kid's favorite cereal is almost eight dollars a box? It was under four last year."

"I don't know how folks are making it," I tell her. Handing over a twenty, I wonder how much longer my mom and I are going to make it. If she goes into a home, it's going to cost a fortune. And the sale of the house won't cover her care indefinitely.

I chit chat for a couple more minutes before heading over to Higgens'. I promised my mom I'd make some chicken and potato soup. I might even bake a fresh loaf of bread if I'm feeling ambitious.

Grabbing a cart, I push it over to produce where I pick up some onions, celery, carrots, garlic, and fresh ginger. I pass by Emmy Roberts who works at the local bookstore, Falling for

Books. Like me, she's a caretaker. But in her case, she takes care of her grandmother, which seems way more normal at our age. I'd stop to say hello, but Emmy appears to be totally engrossed by her shopping list.

I veer my cart around to the back of the store to get a whole chicken. I'll roast the bones before adding it to the broth, not only for the extra flavor but extra vitamins that will leach out. That's where I run into Zach. He's talking to Bennet, the butcher.

He asks, "Do you have any Prime steaks?" Bennet looks at him like he's off his meds.

"I don't even have Choice," he tells Zach. "If you're looking for Prime, you've got quite a drive ahead of you." When Zach doesn't respond right away, Bennet offers, "But if you want something delicious, I've got some amazing Chinook. It just came in this morning."

Zach nods his head. "I do love salmon. I'll take four pounds."

"Four pounds of salmon?" I demand from behind him. He practically jumps out of his skin.

"Is that a problem?"

I look at the twenty-four dollar a pound price tag and then back to him. Who *spends a hundred bucks on fish for one person?* "I guess if you don't mind eating it day and night until you've finished it …" He and I clearly live on different planets.

Bennet wraps the gorgeous fillets in white paper and hands them over to Zach before asking me, "What can I get for you, Ellie?"

I try to do a Vulcan mind meld on Zach and will him to walk away, but it doesn't work. So, I tell Bennet, "I need a whole chicken, but it doesn't have to be a big one."

It's no secret that my mom and I aren't loaded, so he smiles knowingly while saying, "I've got some dark meat parts on the bone for a fraction of the cost. You want those?" While I wish he didn't have to say this in front of Zach, I'm not so high in the instep that I don't appreciate a bargain. "That's perfect, Bennet. The dark meat will taste great in my soup."

Bennet used to be friends with my dad when he was alive. He tried to keep up with my mom, but her health took such a turn that she doesn't see many people anymore. After wrapping up my order, he hands it over. "Give your mom my best, will you?"

I agree to do that while taking the package from him. Walking away, I tell Zach, "I just need to get some yeast and then I'm done. Should I meet you in the car?"

"How about walking around with me and showing me where everything is?"

I'm about to tell him I don't know where they keep the caviar, but I think better of it. Instead, I investigate his cart and ogle the healthy selections, before asking, "What else do you need?"

"Frosted Flakes, milk, and ice cream."

"Frosted Flakes?" I giggle.

"Is there something wrong with that?"

Pushing my cart toward the cereal aisle, I tease, "I took you more for a Raisin Bran kind of guy."

"Why in the world would you think that?" Good, he's taken the intended offense.

I shrug my shoulders. "Raisin Bran seems sensible and grown up. Frosted Flakes is kind of childish." He looks stunned at my assessment but doesn't comment on it. I tease, "What kind of ice cream do you get? Bubblegum?"

"Very funny. I'll have you know I like butter pecan, mint chocolate chip, and pistachio."

"What about cookie dough? That's my favorite."

"I've never had it," he says.

I stop walking so I can shout right at him. "You're kidding?"

"No."

"Zach, your nephews practically live on cookie dough ice cream. In fact, you should probably get them some while you're here."

"Fine. I'll get them some and I'll get me some. I'll let you know my verdict."

Even though I don't want to talk to Zach all the time, I realize I won't be able to keep my distance entirely. I mean, in addition to staying in a cottage on the same property I am, he's sure to be at the ice rink a lot. "You'll like it," I assure him.

"What if I don't?" The grin on his face makes it clear he's teasing.

"You will."

Zach and I continue our stroll through the aisles, which feels uncomfortably domestic. It's the kind of thing I'd do with a boyfriend or husband, not a tenant.

After paying for our stuff, we drive back to the house. I tell Zach, "I need to check on my mom and then go back to the rink for my last lesson of the day. I got most of the inside of your place cleaned, but I'll have to stop by tomorrow and pick up the curtains for washing."

"What about the windows?" he wants to know.

"The windows are *your* job."

"I thought you had to approve of my work before allowing me to stay tonight," he says playfully.

I don't take the bait. "At this point, the place is yours for two months. Wash the windows, don't wash the windows. I don't care."

As I walk towards the front door of my mom's house, he calls out, "I'll let you know about the ice cream!"

I wish he wouldn't. While Zach and I had a nice enough day—considering I tried to pick a fight with him through most of it—I really don't need to get to know him any better.

The last thing I want is to fall for a spoiled rich guy who has the world at his feet.

CHAPTER NINE

Zach

I'm not sure what lessons I'm supposed to have learned from the past few months, but it's clear I've learned nothing about women. Seriously. I thought I'd broken the ice with Ellie—if not at the diner, then at the market. But now that we're back to her place— boom! The ice princess is back.

Instead of carrying my groceries all the way back to the cottage, I decide to go over to Troy's and spend time with the boys. Terry is the oldest at nine. Then there's Trent who's eight, Travis is six, and Tommy just turned two.

I don't really get the whole naming everyone with the same initial craze, but that might have more to do with my name beginning with a Z. Even though my favorite Dr. Seuss name starts with a "Z"—Zanzibar Buck Buck McFate—the rest of my options would be limited.

Knocking on the door, I call out, "I have cookie dough ice cream!" I hear the shouts of excitement long before the door opens. When it finally does, Kelly is standing there holding the baby under one arm like the expert wrangler of boys that she is.

"Zach!" She puts Tommy down before wrapping her arms around me. "We're so glad you're here."

I hug her tightly before lifting her up, so the top of her head meets my chin. "Even though I came early?"

"So long as you don't mind pizza delivery for supper," she says.

I look behind her to the four little bodies waiting for an invitation to say hello. "I bought salmon at the market. I didn't want to come empty handed."

After putting my sister-in-law back onto her feet, I bend onto one knee and open my arms to my nephews. Terry and Trent have known me the longest, so they're the first to charge. Travis and Tommy aren't far behind.

Terry jumps on me and knocks me to the ground. "Uncle Zach, where have you been?"

Trent is next. "Did you bring presents?"

Travis piles on. "I heard something about ice cream."

I rough house with the older boys for a few minutes while answering their very important questions. "I've been working my butt off; I brought Kings sweatshirts; and most importantly, the ice cream is in the car. You all need to get your shoes on and go unload the groceries."

As the big kids run away, Tommy steps forward and demands, "Who you?"

"This is your uncle Zach," Kelly tells him. "You were just a baby the last time you saw him."

Tommy tips his head to the side and studies me closely. "Unca Zach?"

"That's me." I reach out a hand to him.

Instead of taking it, he walks toward me and lifts his arms into the air to be picked up. My heart melts. While I have little exposure to children, I really do love my nephews. Picking up Tommy, I tell his mom, "I'll cook tonight. Troy can clean up."

"Whatever will I do with so much free time?" I can't tell if she's joking.

"You could take a bath or go to bed early."

"You really don't know anything about being a parent, do you?" She takes in my perplexed look and laughs before explaining, "Making supper is the easiest part of being a mom." As her older sons come charging back into the house with grocery bags, she explains, "The hardest part is keeping all the toys picked up, the bedrooms cleaned, and endeavoring to keep these rascals semi-clean."

"I'll help," I volunteer. I mean, how hard can little boys be? It seems I've forgotten the amount of chaos my brothers and I were capable of as kids.

Once the groceries are inside, I ask, "Who wants ice cream?" A barrage of enthusiasm ensues.

"After supper!" Kelly yells over the noise.

Terry tries to negotiate for the boys. "This is a special occasion, Mom."

"Pleeeeease," Travis and Trent add.

It isn't until Tommy offers his, "PEEEEEEES," that Kelly concedes.

"Fine, but just this once. Uncle Zach will be here for two months, so tonight is the only special occasion night." She eyes them so closely you'd think she was inspecting them for lice. "Agree to my terms," she orders.

After three, "Yes, Moms," and one "Yummy, ice cream!" I lead the boys to the kitchen. Kelly puts out bowls while I fill them.

Putting two scoops in each dish, I announce, "A little birdie told me you like cookie dough ice cream the best."

"What bird?" Trent sounds confused.

"Yeah, birds don't talk," Travis confirms. "Unless it was a parrot, but we don't know any parrots."

"Ellie Butler told me," I explain.

The boys look at me like I'm nuts for referring to Ellie as a bird, but their attention is soon diverted by carrying their bowls to the kitchen table.

Kelly looks intrigued. "So, you've met Ellie. She's great, isn't she?"

"She's something," I say. Kelly quirks an eyebrow, so I explain, "The only way she'd let me move in a day early was if I agreed to wash the windows of her cottage."

Kelly valiantly tries not to laugh in my face. "You could have stayed here," she says before teasing, "I would have only made you shampoo the carpets."

I pick up my ice cream off the counter and take it to the table to sit with the kids. Lifting my spoon, I announce, "I've never had cookie dough ice cream." Four sets of brown eyes turn to me in shock, so I explain, "I'm more of a butter pecan kind of guy."

"That's what Dad eats," Terry says with his mouth full.

"Speaking of Troy, where is he?" I ask.

"Probably up at the lodge making sure everything is ready for his team," Kelly says. "He's pretty excited."

"I hear it's a great crew," I say before taking a bite from my dish. The base is vanilla but there are chunks of actual cookie dough—holy yum!

"It really is. Troy got Dan Roberts, one of the guys from his old team, others he knew from the Olympics and then there were referrals. Dan recommended a buddy from his college days named Dawson. And you know your brother. He's trying to jump start the career of a couple of guys who fell off the radar. The assistant coach is a former star who left the ice because his wife passed away."

The last comment hits hard. I can't imagine having a spouse yet, let alone losing her. "It sounds like Troy is planning to raise a sizable amount, if he thinks he can match my two mil with corporate sponsors."

Kelly nods her head. "He's hoping to inspire people to become more charitable. So many folks sit around feeling so overwhelmed they can't solve the big problems of life, they forget that if we all did something, no matter how small, the big problems wouldn't be nearly as daunting."

Troy and Kelly have always been community minded. They're true inspirations. "That's a good way of looking at things."

Once we've finished our ice cream, I tell the older boys to go grab a ball so we can go outside and throw it around for a bit.

Travis shakes his head. "We'd rather go to the rink."

"We're really good," Terry says. "But we're not ready to turn pro yet." I love that they have such big dreams, but I can't imagine anything else with the parents they have.

"You should probably grow up first," I tease.

"Duh, but you know how it is, Uncle Zach. You've got to spend every free minute on the ice if you want to become a legend like 'Dan the Man' Roberts," he proudly boasts, naming the local Maple Falls guys who made it to the NHL. "That's what I'm gonna be—a legend."

"Not a legend like your dad, huh?" I tease him.

A grimace crosses my nephew's face. "Dad was great and all, but Dan is still doing it, you know?"

"I know," I tell him. I remember being just as excited as he is when I was a kid. It never occurred to me my career would get cut short just as it was taking off. Looking over at Kelly, I tell her, "I can take the three older boys if you're good with that."

"You can't take us without Tommy," Terry says. "He skates better than he walks." Kelly nods her head to confirm the truth of her eldest's statement.

"Okay," I announce, "everyone who wants to go to the rink, get your skates!"

Kelly stands up and removes a set of keys from a hook on the wall. "You might as well take my minivan. That way you don't have to move the baby's seat."

"Are you really trusting me with all four boys?" I ask in shock and not a small amount of fear.

"You bet I am. The older three know the routine. Just keep your eye on Tommy. He's a bit of a wildcard."

I'm suddenly not so sure I'm up for this trip. Looking down at my youngest nephew, I ask, "Are you going to be good for Uncle Zach?"

He smiles brightly before answering, "No."

With panic etched across my features, I look at Kelly and practically beg, "Please come with us."

Instead of agreeing, she says, "I can't take a bubble bath at the rink."

"Maybe you can take your bath tonight?"

She shakes her head. "No, thanks."

"Kelly …" My voice nearly shakes in panic.

Reaching out, she punches my shoulder and says, "You got this, big guy. After all, you grew up with four brothers."

And just like that, beads of sweat appear on my forehead. I did grow up with four brothers and we were nothing short of terrors on—and off—the ice.

CHAPTER TEN

Ellie

After I hand my mom a pain pill with a glass of water, she grumpily tells me, "This is going to put me right to sleep again."

I sit down on the couch next to her chair. "Our new tenant is going to give you some turmeric to try for the inflammation. He says it really helps him."

"Is he eighty?" she jokes.

"Ex hockey player," I tell her. "He had a game-ending injury in college."

Mom swallows her pill. "I didn't think he was coming until tomorrow."

I give her the low down on Zach showing up early, leaving out the part where I made him wash the windows. "I'm off to the rink for another lesson," I tell her. "I'll make supper when I get home."

She shakes her head. "Don't bother, I'll be sleeping." Pushing the remote on her lift chair, she asks, "Can you help me get into bed before you go?"

A wave of sadness rolls over me as I slowly guide her to the back of the house and tuck her in. The tables have turned in a big way. Being able-bodied sometimes makes me feel like I'm more of a mother than daughter. As I plug my mom's phone into the charger on the nightstand, I tell her, "Call if you need anything."

"Got it." She rolls over and pulls her down comforter over her shoulders. Then she closes her eyes and goes to sleep. *What kind of life is this for her?* I wish I could talk Mom into letting me get her out more, but she's so convinced she's a burden, she won't let me. The isolation is making her depressed. But then again, I'm sure her inability to get around independently has a lot to do with that as well.

When I walk out the front door, I notice Zach's SUV is gone. He probably went over to Troy's house, which is fine by me. In fact, it would be great if he changed his mind about needing quiet and decided to stay there. In this scenario, I would still charge him two months' rent for all the aggravation he's caused me. Yet if I'm being honest, I'm not sure it's been nearly as bad as I'm making it out to be.

As I drive to the rink, I replay scenes from the afternoon in my head. Had I never heard those reports about Zach, I wouldn't have guessed he was the same guy the media portrays him to be.

Having said that, I'm not so naïve as to blindly trust him. Being Troy's brother isn't enough of a reason to accept him at face value.

I'm running a few minutes behind schedule, so by the time I get inside and put my skates on, my entire class has already assembled. I loved skating when I was a kid, and even though I can't do all the jumps, I'm still a credible instructor for beginners.

"Ellie!" Teah Randolph calls out. "Can I do an axel today?" Her eyes dart to the left.

Following their direction, I see what's got her so amped up. Troy and Kelly's oldest is nearby. "Terry Hart, huh?"

Teah's smile is blinding. "He's so cute, Ellie."

"And you want to show him what a great figure skater you are." Her blonde curls bob up and down in excitement, so I tell her, "Sure, but let's do it at the end of the class when you're good and warmed up."

"Yes!" She raises one fist victoriously in the air while skating away to join the rest of her class. Meanwhile I look around for Kelly—she sometimes brings the kids at night to wear them out before bed. But instead of seeing her, I spy Zach. He's standing on the rink in a pair of hiking boots trying to chase after Tommy—or the ice devil, as I like to call him.

Gliding out in front of my class, I tell them, "Give me two minutes. While I'm gone, go ahead and practice your figure-eights." Zach doesn't see me until I bend down and scoop up Tommy for him.

"Ellie, hi." He looks frazzled.

"You've got to put on skates to keep up with this one," I tell him.

"I don't skate anymore."

"You're less likely to fall on skates than with street shoes. Tommy's got some speed in those little feet." Tommy looks up and me and pulls on my hair. "Hey, big guy," I tell him.

"Ellie, Ellie, put me down!" he shouts. "Wanna go!"

"As soon as your uncle puts his skates on," I tell him.

"Now!" This little boy is nothing if not determined.

"How about if I take you over to my class while Uncle Zach gets ready?"

"I don't have skates with me," Zach interjects.

"It's an ice arena, Zach. They *rent* them."

He looks about as happy as I do when I borrow shoes at a bowling alley. But I don't take time to commiserate. Instead, I tell him, "Hurry up. Then come over and get Tommy." I point across the rink to my class.

I skate away with Tommy still under my arm while he wiggles to get free. When we get back to my kids, I tell them, "Our first warm up lesson is called, chase the two-year-old." The kids know what that means and they start to laugh. Everyone loves Tommy Hart—in small doses, anyway.

Putting Kelly and Troy's youngest on the ice, I tell him, "Do your best, little guy." Then I set him free.

Tommy darts left where there is an opening, but as soon as my class sees where he's going, they block him. Then the two-year-old moves to the right. Another block. This goes on for ten minutes before Zach finally shows up. Skating easily to my side, he announces, "I'm back."

I point to Tommy. "Good. He's yours now. I have a class to teach."

Yet I'm so distracted staring at Zachary Hart skating with his young nephew, my class pretty much does their own thing. Tommy moves like a bolt of lightning, but every time his uncle catches him, he laughs and squeals like he's having the time of his life. The whole scene is so precious, I'm pretty sure I spontaneously ovulate somewhere along the way.

Towards the end of the class, I pull Teah over to the side and ask, "You think you're warmed up enough for that axel?"

She beams, "I've got this, Ellie."

Teah turns around and skates in Terry Hart's direction. When he sees her, she gives him a flirtatious wave. Then, while she still has his attention, she skates forward, lifts her right knee, and pushes her hands downward before she jumps. Teah spins in the air—not one and a half times as I've taught her, but nearly twice that.

My student lands perfectly on her left foot and finishes with a slight curtsey toward me. "You did a double!" I call out excitedly.

"I've been practicing," she shouts back.

Meanwhile, Terry skates toward my star student and appears to congratulate her. I can't help but smile at how proud Teah seems, not only to have accomplished her goal, but to have caught the eye of her crush.

Looking around for Zach, I find him chatting with Troy. Tommy appears to have finally worn himself out because he's sound asleep on his father's shoulder.

Even though I should probably just leave, my skates have a mind of their own. Before I know it, I'm in full glide in the direction of my tenant. Troy spots me first. "Hey Ellie, how's it going?"

"Good, Troy. How are you?"

"Exhausted." He nuzzles his nose into Tommy's hair before saying, "I forget how grueling a two-year-old can be."

"Tommy is your fourth," Zach tells him. "How many kids do you need to remember?"

"Apparently four." Troy laughs before adding, "Kelly has made it clear that Tommy is our last." He turns his attention to his brother. "It's your turn to bring more Hart men into the world."

Zach looks appalled at the suggestion. "I don't think so."

I want to ask what he has against kids, but I don't want to appear too interested. Instead, I volunteer, "I'm heading home now." Addressing Zach, I add, "I'll be over tomorrow to pick up your curtains for a wash."

Troy surmises, "So he passed the window washing test and you're letting him stay tonight?"

I don't bother explaining that the windows never fully got cleaned. Instead, I tell him, "He's staying."

Troy lightly punches his brother's shoulder. "Looks like if the whole tycoon thing doesn't pan out, you've got yourself a backup career."

"Ha, ha," Zach responds, clearly not enjoying being the butt of a joke.

"Can you find your way back to the cottage?" I ask him. Even though I don't want to spend more time with the man, there's a small part of me that can't seem to get enough. I mentally chastise myself for even admitting such a horrible truth.

"I think I can manage," he says. "However, if you *want* me to come with you ..."

Before he can finish that sentence, I assure him, "I'm good, thanks." Turning to Troy, I add, "I'll be over tomorrow to help Kelly get the welcome baskets ready for the players." He nods his head.

"That's a nice touch," Zach says. "What are you putting in them?"

Troy answers, "Just the basics. A brochure of Maple Falls and all the fun things going on here in the autumn, a t-shirt with our Ice Breakers slogan on it, a couple bottles of water, and a commemorative hockey puck."

When he's done, I add, "Energy bars, a jar of nuts, custom-made soap that smells like maple syrup, and Kelly's homemade Rice Krispie treats." I explain to Zach, "She doubles the amount of marshmallows and butter."

Zach groans low in his throat which causes a butterfly effect in my stomach. Like seriously, it feels like there are a million of them flapping away in search of freedom.

"Oh, I know Kelly's Rice Krispie treats," he says. "I'll have to make sure I'm around when you gals are packing everything up." *Why did I say anything about those treats?* The last thing I want is to spend more time with Zach Hart.

"I'll bring that turmeric by for your mother tomorrow," he says.

"Thanks." So much for hating the guy completely. Waving to the Hart brothers, I skate off the ice, yet my gaze can't seem to stay in front of me. I keep looking back at Zach like we're opposite sides of a magnet.

I continue to stare at him while taking off my skates. I consider that he may not be the fiend the media portrays him to be. Or maybe he's just a good actor. I've been watching Yolanda Simms on television for years and I can't imagine she's lying about his character. She's just too credible—she's too much of a woman's woman to lie about a dog like him.

An image of Zach leaving Shirley May what was probably the biggest tip of her life creeps in. I question whether he did that for my benefit and a new wave of irritation washes over me. I force myself to break this hold he has on me and turn to storm out of the arena.

Zach Hart is nothing more than an entitled self-serving player and nothing will convince me otherwise. That's what I'm telling myself, anyway …

CHAPTER ELEVEN

Zach

After tonight's adventure with my brother's kids, I deduce parents must be bionic. How they manage those rug rats on top of all the responsibilities they have keeping a family afloat is beyond me.

By the time I get back to my little cottage in the woods, it's all I can do not to flop into bed still wearing my clothes. Somehow, I find the energy to brush my teeth, change into pajama pants, and crawl between the sheets before I lose consciousness. Yet by the time I'm nestled in, my brain gets a second wind and starts churning like I'm destined to take the blue ribbon at a butter-making contest at the state fair.

My biggest concern is Yolanda coming to Maple Falls. She can only have one agenda and that's to make my life unbearable. *What did I ever do to that woman other than correct her assumption about our relationship?* She's clearly dated enough men to know that what we had was nowhere near committed, nor was it a relationship, for that matter.

The truth is that famous people dating each other is often nothing more than a PR arrangement made to give both parties the kind of press they're looking for. In my case, that was done in hopes that Yolanda would assure the public I was a decent guy, not the opposite. In fact, that had been our agreement to the letter.

Yolanda's boon was being seen in public with me. And while that may sound egotistical, being aligned with the CEO of a *Fortune* 500 company has a way of opening doors that otherwise remain closed. Yolanda was using my clout to blast through any obstacle that stood in her way.

Even though our first date was arranged by Fame, Inc.—the company that handles both of our PR needs—she decided to deviate from the script. While technically I could just return her call and find out what her terms are, I can't for the life of me imagine I would give in to her terrorist demands and let her win this unjust attack. In fact, quite the opposite. She's declared war on my character, and I'm not going to settle for anything short of total redemption.

Picking up my phone, I set my alarm for my standard five a.m. While I'd love to sleep in, I'm going to get up and finish the window washing so that when Ellie shows up to get the curtains, everything is sparkling. I don't bother facing the truth of my motivation, which is to see my landlady smile. Instead, I tell myself it's because I hate when people think I'm one of the idle rich. Just because I've made a fortune doesn't mean I'm incapable of performing basic tasks.

Closing my eyes, I envision Ellie at the skating rink. She's got a squirming Tommy under her arm and she's effortlessly skating away with him. God clearly knew what he was doing when he created such a glorious woman. Ellie is feisty, fiery, and full of righteousness. Being around her is like standing in the middle of a storm with no idea how hard the wind is going to blow or where the next lightning strike is going to land. Plainly put, she's a force to be reckoned with and I find her irresistible.

Nearly an hour passes before my brain finally turns off and allows me to rest. I don't require eight hours of sleep, or even seven, but six is always appreciated.

When my alarm rings, my eyes pop open and for a split second, I can't remember where I am. After turning off the Wagner's "Ride of the Valkyries"—or Elmer Fudd's "Kill the Wabbit" music, as I first learned of it—my phone rings. I answer before looking at caller ID. "Hello?"

"Get up." It's Belle.

"What's with the wake-up call?" I ask. This is not the norm in our relationship.

"Yolanda's on a plane. She arrives in Maple Falls at seven o'clock this morning."

"Why? Practices don't start for two more days."

"The station claims she wants to be there and get set up before the players arrive, but we know the truth. She wants to get there and catch you unaware."

"If the station told you she's coming today, she has to know that I know what she's up to."

Belle feigns a heavy Southern accent. "Sugar, I don't know what you're talking about. No one told little Annabelle Barnes anything about you. They told Belle McCallister, assistant to the event coordinator of Ice Breakers, where their turkey is flying."

Laughter erupts out of me. "Belle, you are seriously the best assistant I've ever had."

"And the best you ever will have, so don't get any ideas about replacing me anytime soon."

"Never," I assure her. "But it probably won't be too long before KBIZ figures out there's no Belle McCallister associated with the event and your insider info will dry up."

"True," she says. "But until then, I suggest you prepare yourself to come face-to-face with the antichrist."

"Is she staying at the lodge?"

"She has a room booked for the full six weeks."

"Why so long? It's just a bunch of charity hockey games, for Pete's sake. In the land of television news, that can't be more than three or four ninety-second reports, which certainly does not warrant such an expense."

"I don't know, Zach, but if I were you, I'd put on my big boy pants and prepare to find out."

I exhale the air from my lungs, hoping to push out the feeling of impending doom that's building inside of me. "Thanks for the heads up," I tell Belle. "Call me if you learn anything else."

"I'm guessing at this point you'll find out before I do. Keep me apprised so I can create a battle plan."

Throwing the covers off my legs, I ask, "Has Pinky been in touch yet?" Pinky Albright is my publicist who has been surprisingly unresponsive since Yolanda went rogue.

"Nothing yet, but I'll put in another call this morning."

"If she won't talk to you," I say, "tell her secretary I'm dissolving our contract due to negligence."

"Done. In the meantime, Zach, stay out of trouble and don't let Yolanda bait you."

"I'll do my best," I tell her before ending the call. I get up, brush my teeth, and put on a t-shirt before turning on the coffee. While I wait for it to brew, I fill the bucket with hot soapy water and take it outside. I proceed to channel my frustrations by scrubbing down the remaining three windows.

Once that task is accomplished, I go inside and drink two cups of coffee, then I spend the next two hours making sure the interior windows in Ellie's cottage sparkle like they're brand new. I'm finishing the final one when I spot my landlady strolling down the path.

Hurrying to change shirts, I leave my pajama pants on in a bid to look like I haven't been up for hours cleaning. I open the door as soon as I hear her knock. "Good morning," I tell a refreshed-looking Ellie. She is seriously one gorgeous woman. And tall. I like being able to look a woman in the eye.

Her eyes shift around me like she's valiantly trying not to make eye contact. "Good morning."

Tipping my head to the side so she can't look away without making it obvious, I ask, "Would you like a cup of coffee? I'm about to put on a new pot."

"No, thank you." Her eyes dart toward the curtains she still needs to take down. "I'm just here to get the drapes." That's when she notices the windows. "You washed them?" She sounds so surprised you'd think I'd built an entire house with my own two hands.

"I did."

"Why?"

"Because I didn't want you crying foul on our bet."

A small smile crosses those luscious lips of hers. "Too cheap to pay an extra month's rent, huh?"

Shaking my head, I confess, "Too proud to have you think I wasn't capable of basic chores."

That seems to take her off guard. "Why do you care what I think?"

Taking a step closer, I ask, "Why wouldn't I?"

She ducks around me and heads toward the windows. "Don't play games with me, Zach. I'm not in the mood."

"I'm not playing games." I seriously have no idea why this woman hates me so much. Unless she's so gullible that she believes everything she hears on television.

Ellie gathers the curtains and strides purposefully toward the door. "I'll bring these back later today." And then, like a jackrabbit pursued by a hungry fox, she hightails it back up the path.

I don't have time to try to figure out why she has a bee in her bonnet. Instead, I fix myself a quick breakfast and get dressed for the day. If Yolanda is arriving this morning, I need to get to the rink and stake my territory.

The first thing I need to do is make sure I have a key to the office, so I have sanctuary whenever I need it. The second item on my agenda is to think of a way to keep Yolanda in check, so she doesn't make my public life any more miserable than she already has. Given the damage she's already done, I do wonder at my chances.

CHAPTER TWELVE

Ellie

I blame my sorry lack of a social life for my inability to keep my cool around Zach. Once again, I nearly drooled all over the man. It didn't hurt that he did such a great job cleaning those windows —I've always considered men doing housework highly attractive. Having said that, I don't need any more reasons to want to climb Zachary Hart like a ladder that leads to an all-you-can-eat french fry buffet.

I hurry back into the house and toss Zach's curtains into the wash before waking my mom. I bring her a bowl of her favorite oatmeal combo—steel-cut oats, flavored with peanut butter, cinnamon, and candied ginger. "Good morning," I sing as I open her blinds. "How did you sleep?"

Mom rolls over but doesn't open her eyes. Checking her pain meds, I notice the cap is ajar. She can no longer screw on lids and caps—a byproduct of her crippled joints. As such, I deduce she needed extra pain meds in the middle of the night. Being that I don't know when she took them, I can't gauge how long she'll sleep.

I write a note for her on the pad of paper she keeps by her

bedside telling her that I'm leaving her breakfast in the kitchen and all she needs to do is pop it in the microwave for forty-five seconds. Then I ask her to text me when she wakes up.

I hate leaving the house while Mom's still in bed, but I'm expected over at Kelly's to fill baskets and I don't want to knock her off schedule.

Saying a silent prayer my mom gets up okay on her own, I grab my purse and head out the door. The air is cooling to the point where I now carry a sweater with me, which is no hardship. Fall is my favorite season. Colorful leaves, the bluest skies you've ever seen, and pumpkin-spice everything. Sign me up!

Zach's SUV is still next to mine, so I hurriedly get into my car. I don't need more interaction with him if I can help it. On the way to Kelly and Troy's, my mind is full of thoughts regarding my boss's insanely rich and handsome brother. Zach is nothing like I expected him to be, which I find highly disconcerting. I thought he'd be arrogant and dismissive, but he's not either of those things. In fact, he seems to want to engage with me, which is causing my blood pressure to rise at an alarming rate.

I pass Troy as I pull into the Harts' driveway. He slows down and opens the passenger-side window. "Morning, Ellie. Kelly was up most of the night with Tommy. The little booger had an upset stomach."

"Too much ice cream?" I guess.

"That might be part of it, but likely the biggest culprit is having eaten a pound of salmon all by himself. That kid has no shutoff valve when it comes to food he loves."

Zach must have brought over the salmon he bought at the store. I don't know why, but that charms and irritates me in equal measure—which appears to be my baseline feeling about the man.

"What about the older boys?" I ask. "Are they up yet?"

"Up and out," he says. "The school is hosting a pancake breakfast and there's no way they were going to miss that."

I'm not surprised to hear this, as the Hart family never seems to rest. "Okay. I'll head in and start assembling. Do you want me to take the baskets to the lodge when they're done?"

"Bring them to the arena. We're going to hand them out after we introduce everyone to the press tomorrow."

Nodding my head, I tell him, "Sounds good."

Troy and Kelly's house is everything I could dream of in a home. It's a huge two-story log house that blends into the landscape so seamlessly it looks like it grew straight out of the ground like a complicated tree. I let myself through the front door without calling out a greeting and head in the direction of the formal dining room where Kelly and I have been collecting basket items.

The baskets are dark-straw weave with a large handle over the top. I start pulling them apart and lining them across the table. Then I put in a royal blue hand towel before placing four bottles of water in the back. I roll the t-shirts next before inserting the food and additional items. Finally, I tuck in all the brochures for fun things our visitors can do in their downtime.

This really is the best time of year to visit Maple Falls. The town's population triples because of the fall festival alone. I mean, who doesn't love music, corn mazes, apple bobbing, and every caramelly treat you can imagine? My favorite is the caramel corn with macadamia nuts and pecans that Shirley May makes. Add to that our killer farmers' market that Kiki runs, and the insanely gorgeous foliage that comes with this time of year, and you can't lose.

I imagine this year's festival is going to be the biggest success ever due to all the well-known hockey players who will be temporarily calling Maple Falls their home. I start to wonder if some hottie might catch my eye, when an image of Zachary Hart pops into my head. I sternly tell myself, *not him!* I want to meet someone eligible—not someone who toys with women like he does.

I finish stuffing the baskets with more force than necessary. So much so, I need to reshape several cereal treats. When I'm done, I tie the blue and red ribbons Kelly and I had previously assembled onto the front of the containers.

Kelly still hasn't come down by the time I'm done, so I take out my camera and shoot an array of pictures to text to her so she knows how nicely our efforts turned out. Then I start taking trips out to my car and fill every inch of open space with hockey swag.

By the time I get to the arena, I'm full of excitement. It's going to be fun being surrounded by famous hockey players and all that entails. I imagine there will be assorted family members, although, according to Troy, only four of the guys on the team are married. The Ice Breakers primarily consist of bachelors, which has the single gals of Maple Falls chit-chatting in overdrive.

There aren't many cars here today because Troy closed the rink to prepare for tomorrow's press conference. Even though he only expects a small number to start, that's sure to grow once the games begin.

When I walk inside, I discover a crew of folks hanging Ice Breaker signs and banners. The team logo is a hockey puck with a broken ice mountain above it. It's really cool.

As I turn to go into the business office, I see Yolanda Simms. I'm about to have a serious fangirl moment and run up to her and tell her how much I love watching her on television, but decide to hold back. There's something about her that doesn't seem all that approachable.

Walking into the office, I flip on the light and proceed to scream like I'm being attacked by a pack of wolves. Zach is sitting in one of the chairs.

He leaps out of the chair before demanding, "What did you do that for?"

"What, scream?"

"Yes." He looks positively wild-eyed like I scared him as much as he scared me.

"Oh, I don't know ..." I drop my purse on the desk across from him. "It might have had something to do with you sitting in a dark office like a predator ready to pounce on your prey."

He runs his fingers through his thick brown hair before sitting back down. "I was thinking."

"In the dark?"

"Why not in the dark?" he demands. "It's more peaceful."

"What could you possibly be thinking about in the dark?" My tone indicates I'm borderline calling him a dullard, as though the man is incapable of intelligent thought.

"If you must know, I'm contemplating an investment I'm about to make."

While the answer sounds plausible, given his business acumen, something in his eyes makes me think he's lying. That's when it hits me. "You're not thinking, you're hiding from Yolanda Simms!"

The faint flush that pops up on his face confirms my suspicion. Yet even so, I'm surprised when he confesses. "So what if I am?"

Laughter booms out of me like a discharging cannon. "Zachary Hart is afraid of the woman he treated like secondhand goods."

His face contorts into an almost hostile glare. "You don't know the facts."

Shrugging, I tell him, "Since you haven't bothered to defend yourself, I just assumed Yolanda was telling the truth."

"I shouldn't have to defend myself when I didn't do anything wrong," he practically hisses.

"Staying quiet makes you look guilty."

"Pleading for my innocence would make me look guilty, too. I'm kind of in a no-win situation, Ellie."

Sitting down on the chair across from him, I ask, "Don't you have people in charge of your press? If you really were innocent, you'd think they'd be helping to make you look better."

"They're the ones who set me up with Yolanda to begin with," I tell her.

"Excuse me?"

"Yolanda and I hire the same PR firm."

My eyes narrow as I ask, "What do you need a PR firm for?"

"I don't need them often," he says, "but I keep them on retainer in case something comes up."

I cross one arm over the other like a genie preparing to grant wishes. "It's almost like you know you're going to get in trouble."

Zach rolls his eyes. "You don't get to be as successful as I am without people causing mischief. It would be stupid not to be prepared."

"And yet here you are," I say. "In trouble and no one is defending you. Like you're guilty of the charges."

Zach stands up and starts pacing back and forth across the room. Given its small dimensions, he can't gain much steam, and winds up resembling a caged tiger.

"I hope no one puts you on a jury anytime soon. You seem to have forgotten that a person is innocent until proven guilty."

He's correct. Yet if he really is innocent, you'd think he'd be shouting his virtue to the rafters. "So, you're saying that you and Yolanda only went out because your PR firm set it up."

"Yes."

"What did you both get out of it?" I want to know.

Zach inhales deeply before releasing his ragged breath. "Yolanda was going to do a flattering interview with me …"

I interrupt, "Because *The Tattler* called you a cheapskate."

He hesitates before agreeing. "Correct."

"What does she get?"

"Great publicity."

"How's that?"

Zach bends down and rests his elbows on his knees. "If I answer that question, you can't hold it against me."

I shrug, neither confirming nor denying my impending reaction.

"Yolanda wants her own national talk show. The network said they would consider it if she could prove she could bring in the kind of big interviews that would promise huge ratings."

His answer confuses me. "Aren't all celebrities media

whores?" I elaborate by asking, "I mean, don't they go on any program that will have them?"

"Not the big names," he says. "They stay selective so that when they're interviewed, it guarantees the eyes of the world are on them."

"If that's true, then why would Yolanda go out of her way to alienate you?"

"It's impossible for me to answer that question."

Standing up from my chair, I walk to the door. With my hand on the knob, I smile brightly. "Why don't we go and ask her?"

I find Zach's look of alarm confusing. If he has nothing to hide, why not confront Yolanda and be done with it?

CHAPTER THIRTEEN

Zach

Ellie and I walk out of the office to find Yolanda standing only a few yards away. A camera operator is next to her with his lens trained directly on us. I feel Ellie's body tense next to mine, so I instinctively reach an arm out to pull her closer to my side.

Meanwhile, Yolanda turns toward the camera and announces, "This is Yolanda Simms reporting from Maple Falls, Washington, where preparations for an all-star charity hockey game are underway to aid underprivileged kids." She turns to me and startles for effect. "And will you look at that. Zachary Hart is here." She strides toward me with purpose as her camera operator trails behind. Stopping in front of me, she demands, "Why are *you* here?" *Like she doesn't already know.*

Had Yolanda been alone, I wouldn't have bothered saying a word to her. But being that she's filming this meeting, that's not an option. "My brother Troy is the one putting this event together," I tell her. "I'm one of the donors."

Yolanda turns her attention toward Ellie, who in turn takes a half step behind me like she's trying to disappear. Yolanda demands, "And who's this?"

"This is Ellie Butler," I tell her. "She's a skating instructor here."

Yolanda rolls her eyes. "Sure, she is."

Ellie steps out from behind me and declares, "I *am* a skating instructor."

"Among other things, I'm sure." Yolanda's insinuation is clear. She thinks Ellie and I are dating.

"I'm also a lifelong resident of Maple Falls," Ellie says.

"And Zach's new *hobby*?"

Ellie's posture straightens like a force from the sky is pulling her ears upward. I'm afraid she's about to say something she'll regret, so I interject, "Ellie and I just met yesterday."

Yolanda eyes her from head to toe before warning, "Before you get any ideas about this man, you should know he's a player. You won't mean anything to him."

I turn to the camera and ask the guy holding it, "Are you still filming this?" He nods his head, so I say, "I'd like to take this opportunity to tell the world that Yolanda Simms and I were set up by our PR team. We have never dated for real. We haven't so much as kissed one another."

Yolanda starts to laugh. "You can forget about anyone ever seeing that little tidbit, Zach. We're not live."

A hot wave of anger warms my cheeks. "And yet, it's the truth, so why are you bent on telling a different story?"

She looks at Ellie before answering, "I'm not going to answer that in front of *her*. I asked you to call me and you haven't."

"I'm happy to leave." Ellie steps forward like she's about to make a break for it. But before she can move out of reach, I stretch my hand out to hers and pull her back.

"Yolanda doesn't have anything to say that I want to hear," I tell her.

"If you don't hear me out," the reporter warns, "I'll double down and make your life more miserable than I already have. You know I can do it."

"Go for it," I tell her.

Yolanda turns to the camera and once again morphs into her sweet TV persona. "You all know what Zachary Hart has done to me, so you must know how hard it is for me to see him again, especially now that he's with another woman. Soon enough you'll learn the degree to which he's betrayed me. Until then, this is Yolanda Simms from Maple Falls, Washington."

Against every impulse to the contrary, I merely walk away. Because I still have a death grip on Ellie's hand, she has no choice but to follow along.

As soon as we're outside, I release her. "I'm sorry about that. You shouldn't have to be a part of whatever Yolanda is trying to pull."

Ellie's brow furrows slightly. "She really hates you. What did you do to her?"

"I already told you, nothing."

She doesn't appear to believe me, but I suppose in her shoes, I might have a tough time as well. Yet it still smarts that Ellie seems more inclined to trust Yolanda than me.

"I'm going to unload the rest of the baskets," she says quietly.

"Please don't talk to Yolanda," I beg her. "Not because I'm afraid of what you'd say, but because of what she can do to you."

The confusion on Ellie's face makes it clear she has no idea the kind of power Yolanda has. "What can she do to me?"

"She can tell lies about you to the entire world. Seriously, Ellie, do not trust her."

Ellie offers a half shrug. "I don't have anything to hide, Zach."

"Yolanda specializes in lies."

Ignoring my warning, Ellie says, "I'll bring your curtains over later this afternoon. If you're not there, can I just take them in?"

"Sure," I tell her. "I don't have anything to hide either."

Ellie's gaze narrows to the point where it feels like she's trying to see inside my soul. "Then you shouldn't be worried about anything."

How can she be so naïve? The truth rarely wins, especially for public figures. Hollywood is nothing but a giant illusion meant to create a narrative to keep people entertained while lining the pockets of the studios. The press is their handmaiden.

I try one last time. "Please be careful, Ellie. I know how to handle Yolanda. You don't."

"Good thing I don't live a life where I have to *handle* people then. I'm not a child, Zach." Oh yeah, she's mad.

I watch as she walks toward her car. While I'm tempted to help her bring the baskets in, I know she doesn't want me around. Also, I don't need to give Yolanda any more footage of me and Ellie together.

After walking around the back of the building, I call Troy. He didn't answer earlier when I tried to alert him the press had already arrived, but he answers now. "Hey, bro. What's up?"

"Yolanda Simms is here, and she's bent on causing trouble."

"What happened?"

"I was hiding in your office when Ellie came in. When we walked out, Yolanda pounced."

"There's nothing to do but face her head-on," Troy says. "You've had enough exposure to the press to know that." He sighs loudly. "We all have."

My brother has had his own run-ins with persistent reporters when he played for the Chicago Blizzard. Several of the players were accused of sexual misconduct by a hotel housekeeper and subsequently became the focus of a nasty investigation.

The housekeeper's lawyer agreed to settle the case for five million dollars, but Troy wouldn't go for it. He said that he didn't do anything wrong, and he wouldn't let people think he'd had any part in such a heinous crime. Troy's teammates, who also claimed innocence, felt accusations like the ones they were facing came with the game, and they just wanted them to go away.

Because Troy wouldn't play ball, the investigation became fodder for the international media, and the reports were salacious at best. The housekeeper didn't go to the hospital after the supposed attack, so there was no DNA evidence. Yet, she had severe bruising and an apparent affinity for acting. So much so, the entire world was ready to convict the players without any proof.

Luckily, Kelly also worked for the hotel—this was before she and Troy met. She overheard some valuable information. The housekeeper was dating a bartender who got drunk one night and boasted to his co-workers that he had come up with a brilliant scam that was about to pay off. He claimed to have coerced his girlfriend into pretending to be victimized by teammates from the Blizzard, so they could make a fortune and move to the Caribbean.

Kelly asked for details and learned that Tanya had just gotten word that without Troy's consent, the club was going to pay her off to make the whole story go away. Kelly didn't know what to do with the information, so she contacted the press and told them what she'd heard. When the police brought the boyfriend in for questioning, he folded like a house of cards in a tornado.

After having his name cleared, Troy wrote Kelly a letter thanking her for her courage. That led to them becoming friends, and when Troy's team went back to Minneapolis to play, he and Kelly had their first date.

"I'm starting to realize how hard your ordeal with the press was," I tell my brother.

"Hockey players are notorious for their bad behavior," he says. "But I wasn't going to be painted with that brush. And *you* shouldn't let the press pigeonhole you either."

"I won't. I just hate that people are so ready to believe the worst."

"Most people look at guys like you and me and think that because we have money and fame, we don't have any problems. That makes them jealous and eager to find a reason to hate us. Sadly, that's just human nature."

"Yolanda has money," I remind him.

"Yolanda is a woman. She's part of a demographic that hasn't always been on the receiving end of fair treatment."

"That's not the case here."

"I didn't say she was a good person. She's clearly taking advantage of past inequality."

"Women should be appalled by what she's doing."

"And they will be if you're able to keep your cool long enough for the truth to come out."

I sound like a real Eeyore when I moan, "I just wish I knew how to make people believe me."

"Trust me, Zach. Yolanda is the kind of person who will eventually hang herself. You just have to give her enough rope."

I know he's right. I just hate sitting around and waiting for her to try to bring me down. "Is there a back entrance to this place that's unlocked?" I ask my brother.

"The players' locker room door is open," he says. "It's about a third of the way around the building, east of the entrance."

"Thanks. I'll be right in," I tell him. And then out of nowhere an idea starts to form how I can make people see the truth about Yolanda. The only hitch is that I'll need a little help from Ellie, and I'm not sure she'll be interested in taking part.

CHAPTER FOURTEEN

Ellie

I feel Yolanda's eyes boring into me as I retrieve the swag baskets for the players. She's vastly different in person than her television persona would lead a person to believe. It's hard to reconcile her being the same person.

As I bring in the last four baskets, the reporter walks over to me. "Need some help?" Even though her tone is friendly, after our last interaction I'm super cautious. "I'm good, thanks."

"I'm sorry about how I acted earlier," she says. "Zach just brings it out in me."

Yolanda is still at my side when I walk into the office and put down my final load. I turn to her and respond, "Zach said you're making everything up. He said your PR team set you up."

She shrugs nonchalantly. "In positions like ours, PR people are our dating apps. Our reps know what we want, and they facilitate our desires." The look on my face must be one of horror, because she hurries to add, "Timothee and Kylee started as a PR couple. Then there's Taylor and Travis, Kim and her second husband, Brad and Jen, and let's not forget Nick and Priyanka. Just because couples meet through their reps doesn't mean they aren't real couples."

I guess I can understand that. "But you and Zach only went out three times," I tell her. "How does that make you a couple?"

"What does the number of dates have to do with anything?" she asks. "People sleep together before they even go on one date. They run off and elope in Vegas after two. Three dates are a lifetime when you're in the public eye."

Ew. But I don't say that. Instead, I go with, "It's none of my business either way. I'm not dating Zach and I'm not interested in dating him." A tiny voice inside my head accuses, *Liar.*

"Then you wouldn't be opposed to helping me out?" The look in her eyes makes my blood run cold.

"I don't want to get involved," I tell her. "My life keeps me plenty busy without looking for additional drama."

"Even if I paid you?" She must sense my desperation for funds, because she clarifies, "Say, ten grand for a month of work?" She explains, "I need an ally here for when I'm back in LA."

Ten thousand dollars is an astounding amount of money. Not only would it get my mom a tricked-out motorized wheelchair, but it would also go a long way in making some long-overdue repairs to our house. Yet, there's no way I'd feel good about taking money that might do someone else harm. And I'm not convinced that isn't what Yolanda is after. As much as it hurts, I tell her, "I'm good, thanks."

She looks beyond surprised. "How about twenty thousand?"

My jaw drops open like a mounted fish. "Dollars?"

"For one month," she repeats.

I don't know whether to believe Zach or Yolanda, but I'm pretty sure I'm leaning toward Zach. No one offers twenty K for help if they have the truth on their side. "I appreciate the offer, Yolanda, but I really don't want to get involved."

Her eyes narrow like she's trying to decide if I'm for real or not. "Don't answer me yet," she says. "Let's wait a few days and see if you feel the same way."

I don't know what she thinks will change my mind, but even if Zach is a real heel, I don't want any part of this. "I don't need to wait," I tell her. "I've made up my mind." As I turn to walk out of the office, I can't help but wonder if I've just made a world-class enemy. The thought causes the little hairs on the back of my neck to stand at attention.

After Yolanda follows me out of the office, I lock the door. Then without another word, I scurry out of the building like Ring-wraiths are chasing me.

Once I'm in my car, I check the time and discover it's already past eleven. I look at my phone and don't see any texts from my mom, which causes a bit of worry. Pulling out of my parking spot, I make short work of driving the few miles home.

After sticking my key into the lock, I swing open the front door of our house only to find the living room empty. The lights are all out and my mother isn't sitting in her lift chair. "Mom?" I call out.

When there's no answer, I yell louder, "Mom! Where are you?"

I hurry down the hall to her bedroom, but she's not in her bed. Real panic overtakes me as I cross the carpet to the bathroom. That's where I find her. My mother is lying on the floor looking like a discarded rag doll. I gently touch her arm and shake her slightly, "Mom, it's Ellie. Are you okay?"

She moans before trying to turn over. "Ellie …" I'm beyond relieved to hear my name. I was terrified she was dead.

"Don't move, Mom. Just stay where you are."

"So cold," she says.

I hurry out of the room and grab a throw off her bed. Going back to the bathroom, I wrap it around her as best as I can. "What happened?" I ask.

She groans again before saying, "I'm not sure. I came in here to go to the bathroom and then when I went to sit on the toilet, I got lightheaded. I must have fallen."

"What time was that?" I ask her.

"About ten."

"Mom, it's after eleven! You've been unconscious for over an hour. We need to get you to the hospital."

Before I can pull out my phone and call 911, I hear Zach call out, "Hello? Anyone home? I've brought the turmeric."

As annoyed as I was at him earlier, I feel nothing but relief now. "Don't move," I tell my mom. "I'll be right back." Then I run down the hall toward Zach.

"Ellie, about this morning …" he starts to say, but I cut him off.

"Forget this morning. My mom fell and I need help getting her into my car so I can take her to the hospital."

He looks alarmed. "We should call an ambulance."

I shake my head. "I can get her there faster."

"That may be, but you don't know how badly she's hurt. Why not let the professionals check her out first?"

I hate having to confess this, but I have no other choice. "The ambulance would probably charge me a thousand dollars to pick her up. We don't have that kind of money."

Instead of looking at me like I'm a monster for placing financial worries above my mom's health, he simply says. "Let me see her."

I lead him into the primary bath, and tell my mom, "This is Zach. He's Troy's brother and the man renting our cottage."

My mom seems to have more of her wits about her because she responds, "I don't normally take visitors in the bathroom." She looks him up and down before appreciatively adding, "But I can make an exception for you."

Zach laughs. "That's very nice of you, thank you."

"Her name is Elaine," I tell him.

"Elaine," Zach says, "do you hurt anywhere?"

"My head hurts," she tells him. "I think I hit it when I fell."

"How about the rest of your body?" he wants to know. "Any pain there?"

My mom gently moves her head from side to side. "No more than usual."

Leaning down, Zach tells her, "I'm going to lift you up and move you to your bed. Is that okay?"

"Yes." I know my mom must be embarrassed to be in this position, but she also seems to know that Zach is more capable of carrying her than I am.

Sliding his arms under my mom, Zach instructs, "Put your hands around my neck."

After getting a closer look at him, she says, "You're very handsome, do you know that?" Now, *I'm* mortified.

"I've been told that," Zach says, "but somehow the compliment means more coming from a beautiful lady like yourself."

My mom actually giggles—giggles!—before deciding, "You're a flirt."

Zach walks across the room and lays Mom down on her bed. Then he looks into her eyes. "You've got some dilation there," he says. "I'm guessing you have a concussion."

"Are you a doctor?" Mom asks him.

"Ex-hockey player from a family of hockey players," he tells her before teasing, "We had more concussions than birthdays." Zach looks at me. "I think we can bypass the ambulance and take her to the hospital ourselves."

"You don't have to come," I assure him.

"I don't, but I'm going to. Do you have a robe you can help your mom into?"

I rush across the room and grab her pink fuzzy bath robe off the back of her closet door. I wrap it around her shoulders before saying, "Really, Zach, just help me get her into my car."

He shakes his head while leaning down to pick my mom up again. "I'm going with you, and I'm driving. That's all there is to it." I'm both relieved not to be alone and irritated by his high-handedness.

Settling into Zach's arms, my mom asks, "Are you single, Zach?"

"I am."

To my eternal horror, she replies, "Good. Ellie's single, too."

CHAPTER FIFTEEN

Zach

Once I get Elaine settled into the back of the Trailblazer, I tell Ellie, "Keep a close eye on her so she doesn't fall over."

"Or vomit all over the back of your truck," she says, suggesting another viable possibility.

"The car is rented, so hurling isn't my concern," I tell her. "I just don't want your mom to hit her head against the window or anything."

Except for Ellie giving me directions to the hospital, we make the short drive in silence. Pulling into the Emergency entrance, I put the car into park before getting out.

"Do you want a wheelchair, Mom?" Ellie asks her.

I interrupt before Elaine can answer. "I'll carry her."

"You can't leave your SUV blocking the entrance."

"I'll take your mom. You move the car." I have Elaine in my arms before she can argue.

Luckily, there isn't much of a line, so I go right to the window and announce, "We need a doctor."

"What happened?" the woman behind the thick glass wants to know.

"She fainted and hit her head. Her daughter says she was unconscious for over an hour." Those are the magic words to get everyone moving in overdrive.

A nurse comes out with a wheelchair and takes Elaine into a triage room while the lady at the desk tells me, "I need to get some information along with an insurance card."

"Her daughter is parking the car, but I'm sure she has everything you need." I remember Ellie saying she didn't have the money to pay for an ambulance, so I add, "If there's no insurance, I'll take care of the bill before we go."

I don't hear Ellie come in, so I jump a little when I hear her say, "My mom has disability insurance." She doesn't make eye contact with me, so I know she's embarrassed by my offer.

I often felt the same way when I was a kid. Too many times I had to decline a party invitation because there was no money for a gift. I didn't go to formal dances in high school because none of us boys had proper suits. Most of the money we made doing odd jobs went to things like school lunches and sports. We even occasionally helped pay an electric bill.

As such, I know Ellie's embarrassment all too well. I would do anything to let her know she never has to feel that way around me.

I wait while Ellie gives the receptionist all the information needed and then I follow her into the triage room. The nurse announces, "Elaine's blood pressure is low, and she's still a little dizzy. We're going to take her straight for a CT scan from here." Looking up from her patient, she tells Ellie and me, "You can sit in the waiting room. Someone will be right out to take you back to her assigned bed."

Ellie leans down and gives her mom a kiss on the cheek before saying, "You've got this, Mom."

"Thanks to you." Then she smiles at me and adds, "And to your friend."

Ellie feels the need to clarify. "He's not my *friend*, he's our tenant." *Ouch.*

I tell Elaine, "I'll be *your* friend, Elaine, even if your daughter won't claim me."

She smiles through a grimace of pain. "I'll take it. Now get going so we can find out how much damage I've done to myself."

I follow Ellie as she walks toward the waiting room. She mumbles, "We may not have much, but we have insurance." Oh yeah, she's ticked off at my offer to pay.

Once we're seated, I ask her, "Do you know anything about Troy's childhood?"

With eyes straight ahead, she answers, "I know he had a great one with a loving family and a load of brothers."

"He did," I concur. "But we were also dirt poor."

She whips her head in my direction with a look of shock etched across her face. "Really?"

I nod. "Really. My parents didn't have college educations and jobs in our town kind of came and went. My dad worked in a series of factories, and my mom took in other people's mending so she could stay home with us boys." Ellie doesn't respond right away, so I ask, "Does that surprise you?"

"Very much. I mean, you guys have everything now. How did you manage that coming from such a start?"

"My folks made our education their biggest priority. They stayed on top of us to get our homework done and they made sure we had a sport we were good at. They tried to negate all obstacles that might have kept us from getting a higher education."

Ellie shakes her head. "You'd think that would be something people would know about you."

"It's not something we hide," I tell her.

After a moment of silence, she confesses, "Things have been tight since my dad died five years ago. He didn't have life insurance and then Covid hit, and nobody came to rent Mom's cottage anymore. That's when her arthritis became debilitating. It was just a lot of tough things hitting at once."

"It's hard to get ahead once the slide starts," I tell her. "I'm sorry you're going through this, but your mom is really lucky to have you."

"I'm lucky to have her," she says. "I know success isn't about how much money you have, but I really wish I had more of it so I could make Mom's life easier."

I reach over and take her hand in mine before giving it a small squeeze. "I get that."

And just like that, Ellie's body relaxes, and she leans toward me. "I have some really great friends," she says. "But everyone has their own lives and I never want them to feel sorry for me. I feel alone a lot of the time."

"Life's burdens can weigh you down," I sympathize. "But the good news is that things always have a way of turning around."

I'm more than a little surprised when she announces, "I'm starting to believe that. Just today, I was offered twenty thousand dollars for a month's work."

"Excuse me?" *Who made an offer like that and what kind of seedy thing do they expect from Ellie in exchange for that kind of money?*

"Yolanda wants me to help drag your name through the mud. At least, I think that's what she's planning." I'm silent for so long, Ellie straightens up and looks at me. "I told her no."

"Why?"

"Are you kidding? Zach, I'm not the kind of person who would take money to help someone hurt you. It may not seem that I like you very much, but it's clear after today you're a decent enough guy."

"Because I brought your mom to the emergency room?" I'm secretly hoping she decided I was a good guy before that.

Nodding her head, she says, "Among other things."

"I have a proposition," I tell her. "I think you should take Yolanda's money and let her think you're on her side."

She looks startled. "But I'd really be a secret agent for you?"

"Yes," I tell her. "And I'll match her twenty thou." Realizing this might be my only chance to help Ellie, I decide, "In fact, I'll double it."

"You want me to take her money *and* yours?" I see a little wheel turning in her head as she tries to compute what she could do with that kind of money.

"You'd be doing me a great favor," I tell her. "I was thinking earlier about asking you to pretend to be Yolanda's friend to get information, but I didn't think you'd go for it."

"Sixty thousand dollars is more than I make in a year." She's so adorably flustered it's all I can do not to wrap my arms around her.

"Does that mean you'll do it?"

"I don't know … I mean … it's just that …" Her poor brain is under assault by all the possibilities. "I'll do it," she finally concedes.

"Good," I tell her. "I'll pay you up front so you can start helping your mom with things she might need. I suggest you get Yolanda to do the same."

"She'd be stupid to give me that kind of money up front. So would you," Ellie reluctantly says.

"Yolanda is desperate," I tell her. "And for some reason she really wants to take me down. I think she'll hand over the money without a second thought."

"Why would *you* trust me?"

"You're a good person," I tell her. "And I have great instincts about people. Also, my brother thinks the world of you, so I know you're a safe bet."

As much as I came to Maple Falls with the sole goal of repairing my reputation, I'm starting to realize there might be another gift to being here. And I'm looking right at her.

CHAPTER SIXTEEN

Ellie

The ER doctor pushes the curtain surrounding my mom's bed to the side before announcing, "The CT scan came back inconclusive. As such, I'd like to keep her overnight to rule out the possibility of stroke." I immediately start to panic. I never considered she might have had a stroke.

Lying on her makeshift bed, my mom tells me, "Go home. I'll be fine."

"I don't want to go home."

"Don't you have lessons today?" she asks.

Shaking my head, I tell her, "The rink is closed today and tomorrow to get ready for the press conference tomorrow."

My mom shifts her attention to the doctor. "You'll call my daughter if you have any concerns, won't you?"

"Of course," she says. "We're keeping you out of an abundance of precaution. We can also help you get around easier here." She smiles at me. "I promise your mom is in great hands and we'll alert you if anything suspicious comes up."

I'm about to tell them that I'm going to stay and nothing they can say will change my mind, when Zach nudges me. He whispers, "We can use the time to get things ready for when your mom comes home."

That's all the encouragement I need. "Fine, Mom, but only if you promise not to be a hero and will call me for any reason. Even if you just want me to make you a sandwich."

Her eyes droop. "I promise. Now, get going."

As Zach and I walk out of the room, I tell him, "I don't like this. I should stay."

"Let's see what changes we can make to your house that will help your mom."

"I already have a bar on her bed. She has a walker and a lift chair. What more can I do?"

"Is there a shower handle?" he asks.

"Yes."

"Is there a toilet seat lift?"

"I didn't even know those were a thing." I briefly wonder if Mom's fall might have been avoided had she not had as far to sit down.

"Let's go to the medical supply store," Zach says. "I'm sure they have a lot of things neither of us know about."

Even though I know that's not his intention, I tell him, "You're making it sound like I've been a bad caretaker."

Leading the way through the automatic doors to the parking lot, Zach says, "Not at all, Ellie. Most people don't know what's out there until they need it. Needs must, you know?" He opens the passenger side door for me. "Where's the store?"

"I don't know." I take my phone out of my purse before asking for the nearest place. I'm not surprised to hear it's thirty minutes away. Maple Falls isn't exactly a big place. "It's a few towns over," I tell Zach. "I can go by myself."

"No way. I'm going with you," he says after getting into the driver's side.

"Why?"

"Why not?"

"Don't you have work to do?" I ask.

"No."

"I find that hard to believe." Although, I am truly grateful for the company, so I don't give him any more trouble.

I turn the radio on to my favorite station and sing along quietly most of the way there. When we pull into the medical supply parking lot, Zach says, "I'll pay for everything today and deduct it from the money I wire to you. Does that work?"

"It does, thank you." I still can't believe he's going to give me such a huge sum to help him. I'll probably give most of it back to him, but first I need to see the kind of damage today's shopping spree is going to cost me.

Walking into the warehouse fills me with excitement. The thought of being able to help my mom without worrying about the cost is a novel experience. The first things I see are hospital beds. I tell Zach, "I've never thought about getting her one of those."

He walks over to the first bed and starts pushing buttons. Not only does the top of the bed lift, but so does the bottom. My favorite part is that the whole mattress raises so Mom can simply lean against it before getting in. Zach signals an employee. "What are we looking at for something like this?"

Tom, according to his name tag, answers, "We rent hospital beds by the month. How long do you anticipate needing one?"

"Forever," I tell him before explaining, "My mom is only in her fifties, but she has crippling arthritis."

He nods his graying head. "In that case, you could probably get insurance to cover it, but these mattresses aren't very comfortable for the long haul. Hang on, I have a catalog you can look at if you want to buy something better."

When he walks away, I tell Zach, "Those beds probably cost a fortune to buy."

"I bet they don't," he guesses.

It turns out Zach is right. I can get a brand-new hospital bed with all the bells and whistles for under two thousand dollars. While that would have been a daunting amount yesterday, I don't blink today.

Zach and I sit down at a nearby table and flip through the catalog. The motorized wheelchairs carry a little more of a sticker shock, but Tom suggests we rent those first so Mom can try out different ones and see which one best suits her needs.

Forty minutes later we leave with a portable wheelchair, toilet lift and guardrails, and shower accessories. For a small extra charge, the bed will be delivered tomorrow.

Once we're back in Zach's car, I tell him, "I couldn't have done this without you. Thank you." Even though my gratitude is real, I still hate feeling like I'm in his debt.

"You're welcome. Now, let's go get lunch."

"You don't need to buy me lunch again."

He smiles before saying, "Then you pay. Where should we go?"

I direct him to a fish house up the road where my parents and I used to go for birthdays. I haven't been in years, so I don't know if it's still good, but I'm looking forward to revisiting some fond memories.

Once we're seated across from each other in a familiar red vinyl booth, I tell Zach, "Their shrimp cocktail is excellent."

"Is that what you always get?"

"I don't come here anymore, but this was my family's special occasion restaurant when I was growing up. That's what I ordered then."

When the waitress comes, Zach and I both order the shrimp cocktail. He adds a Caesar salad for us to split and a basket of garlic bread.

After she leaves, he says, "I don't want you to do anything with Yolanda that makes you uncomfortable. I just want to know what she's plotting."

Nodding my head, I tell him, "That won't be a problem, so

92

long as she tells me. So far, all I know is that she wants me to keep an eye on you and let her know what you're doing."

"Tell her anything and everything. I have no secrets."

"Zach," I start to say before thinking better of it.

"What?"

"Why don't you just hear her out? Then maybe this whole thing would go away."

He takes a sip of water before answering, "I'm not going to give in to her." At my confused expression, he adds, "Once you let someone take advantage of you, they'll just keep doing it. The only way to come out of this intact is to continue to maintain my innocence and not engage with her. People will eventually find someone else to talk about."

"I'd hate to be in your position."

"It's not always easy," he says. "But there's a price to pay for success and this is one of the things I have to deal with."

"What other things do you have to put up with?"

A mischievous smile crosses his face. "Some people think I'm spoiled and entitled, and don't know how to do basic things like clean windows ..."

"I'm sorry about that," I tell him sincerely. "I'm just not used to being around people like you."

Zach shakes his head. "I'm not a trust fund baby, Ellie. I already told you that I grew up with nothing. I know what it's like to struggle."

"I know that now," I tell him. "And I'm sorry I ever thought otherwise."

"Good. Because if we're going to be friends, you have to be able to trust me."

Tipping my head to the side, I ask, "Is that what we're going to be—friends?"

"I'd like that."

"I would, too." Although there's a part of me that would like something more. I wonder what kind of women Zach dates. I'm guessing they're more like Yolanda than me. She's the kind of person that probably spends three hundred dollars on moisturizer and a cool grand on a pair of heels. I wouldn't do that even if I had all the money in the world. At least not if there were people who needed help.

Once our meal is served, Zach says, "Your mom says you're single. Tell me about that."

I nearly choke on a shrimp. "What's to tell?"

He looks at me with laser-like intensity. "Why aren't you dating anyone?"

"Geez, Zach, I don't know. It might have something to do with the fact that I live in a town with very few single men."

"What about the apps? I'm sure there are single guys in nearby areas."

"I'm not a swiper," I tell him prudishly. "Most of those men are just looking for hookups and that's not my thing."

"Good for you," he says. "It's not mine either."

Remembering what Yolanda told me, I say, "You just let your PR people pimp for you, huh?"

He looks surprised. "Excuse me?"

"Yolanda said that people in your position use PR people like dating apps. She said all you have to do is tell them what you want, and they'll set it up."

"That might be what she does," he says. "The only reason I contacted my press agent about Yolanda was to get her to do an interview with me."

"And she wanted more?"

"Apparently," he drawls.

"I'm going to come right out and ask her what she wants from you," I tell him. "I mean, why beat around the bush?"

"We don't want her to suspect you're also working for me," he warns.

"Don't worry, Zach. I'll make sure she knows that I don't like you."

His eyes pop open like he's just had a shock. "But you'd be lying, right? I mean you do like me."

I offer a small grin before saying, "I like you just fine." Even while the words are coming out of my mouth, I know they're a lie. The truth is that I like Zach a lot. I'm just hesitant to give into those feelings because I don't want him to break my heart in six weeks when he leaves Maple Falls for good.

CHAPTER SEVENTEEN

Zach

It's obvious Ellie has thoughts swirling around that pretty head of hers. If I had to guess, I might think they were about me. Although, I'm not sure they would be flattering. For all I know, she still thinks I'm a waste of space.

After paying the check with her credit card, Ellie announces, "I need to go home and get everything ready for my mom."

"I'll help."

Shaking her head, she tells me, "You've done enough, Zach. And while I'm very grateful to you, I want to take care of the rest on my own."

I don't want to push my attentions where they're not wanted, so I simply say, "Fine. But I'm going to help you unload."

As nice as the afternoon has been, it's clear Ellie is done talking. For that reason, I don't try to engage her in conversation on the way back to her house. Instead, I try to figure out what Yolanda wants from me. Short of being in a relationship for real, I come up dry.

Once we get back to Maple Falls, I tell Ellie, "I'll give you my phone number so you can text me." I reach my hand out for her phone and create a contact for myself while adding, "I'll use a code name so that we don't have to worry about Yolanda finding out we're in touch."

Ellie takes her phone back. Looking at the screen, she laughs. "Mr. Wonderful, huh?" She immediately hits the button that calls me and says, "Now you have my number."

I create Ellie's contact, naming her Gorgeous Landlady. "We probably shouldn't be seen together while Yolanda is in town," I tell her.

"And when she's not in town?"

"We should still stay out of the public eye as much as possible. You never know who she has reporting back to her."

"That makes sense." Is it me or does she sound disappointed?

After turning off the ignition, I open the back hatch and take the wheelchair out. Once it's on the driveway, I put all the other purchases on top of it.

"I've got it from here," Ellie says as she maneuvers it toward the front door. She doesn't look back.

I'm not sure what to do now, so I head down to my cottage and give Troy a ring. If he doesn't need me for anything, I might hit that hammock by the creek and take a little nap.

I'm about to call my brother when my phone starts playing "Whip It" by Devo. As my assistant is always cracking the whip, I thought it the perfect tone for her. "Hey, Belle, what's up?"

"You just got a call from Anthony Jenkins."

Tony is one of the partners at Fame, Inc. "Finally, someone is calling me back."

"He gave me his private number and asked that you call him."

"Text it to me," I tell her. Then I tease, "I'm thinking about moving to Maple Falls and falling off the face of the earth."

"Dibs on your condo," she says without missing a beat.

Belle never mentioned whether she was going to take me up on my offer to stay there, so I ask, "Have you moved in?"

"Oh, yeah. I've already put your things into the guest room." I can't tell if she's kidding or not, but knowing her, I wouldn't be surprised if she's done exactly that.

"If I leave California, it's yours," I tell her. "At least until I come back."

Instead of gushing gratitude, she announces, "Your brother Mac called, too. He said to tell you that he needs advice."

"Why didn't he call me directly?"

"He tried to but the call wouldn't go through. It seems Maple Falls has some dead zones."

"Another reason to move here," I joke.

"Haha. That's all I've got for now. Check your texts for Anthony's number." She doesn't bother to say goodbye. Instead, she simply hangs up. That's my Belle, full of charm.

After letting myself into the cottage, I'm suddenly so energized I can't seem to relax. Looking out the back window, I decide to put my swimsuit on and see if the creek is still warm enough to swim in. But the second I walk outside without my clothes on, I change my mind. It looks like living in Southern California for so many years has turned me into something of a wuss.

After putting my jeans and sweater back on, I pick up one of the books I brought with me—*The Reawakening*. It's a blend of conspiracy and apocalyptic fiction, yet the more I read, the more I think it's probably one hundred percent truth and the author was forced to write it as fiction to avoid being sued, or worse, killed.

Once I get to the hammock and lie down, I realize I don't want to read about doomsday. At least not while my mind is so full of thoughts of Ellie. Dropping my book on the ground next to me, I stare up into the colorful leaves above and let my mind drift.

I've worked hard in my life, and I've loved all the stages leading up to the present day. I love the thrill of the chase when I start a new project. I enjoy the feeling of accomplishment when I finish it. I particularly appreciate the fact that I don't have to worry how I'm going to pay my bills. But even though I have a great life, I've recently been realizing that I want more.

I want a wife and a family. I want to recreate my childhood, but with the means to spoil the ones I love instead of struggling. Ellie is once again in the forefront of my brain.

Thinking back to all the women I've dated, I realize that while they have all been beautiful and accomplished in their own way, none of them have inspired thoughts of the long-term. I can't see any of them running around and playing with their kids like my mom did with us—like I instinctively know Ellie would do with her brood.

I don't know if Ellie would welcome romantic attention or not, but I want to let her know that I've started to have feelings for her. I'm not sure if six weeks is enough time for us to form a bond, but I know I want to try.

Thinking of Elaine, I realize that we never know the hand life is going to deal us. As such, I'm going to make the most of every minute that I'm here.

CHAPTER EIGHTEEN

Ellie

I only talked to my mom once yesterday before she fell asleep for the night. Even though she sounded okay, she was very tired. After hanging up, I spent the rest of the day moving her current bed into another room and installing the extra fixtures in the bathroom. Then I rode the wheelchair around the house to make sure it would fit within the existing furniture layout. The only things that needed rearranging were the couch and a couple of side tables.

I went to bed early only to wake up in the middle of the night with my thoughts swirling in a constant loop of my mom, Yolanda, and Zach. What if my mom falls again? What if she has to move into a home? What if Yolanda is right and Zach is a player? I don't bother to pretend that wouldn't hurt because the truth is that I like the guy. A lot.

I finally fell back to sleep, but when I woke up this morning, I felt hungover from the emotional drama of all the what-ifs in my life. After making a pot of coffee, I dig through my purse for the business card Yolanda handed me yesterday. Then I dial the number.

It barely rings before she answers. "Hello?"

"Hi, Yolanda, It's Ellie Butler." She pauses for a minute like she's trying to place me, so I remind her, "From the rink."

"Oh, yes, Ellie!" She sounds more excited than anyone ever is to hear from me. "What can I do for you?"

Inhaling deeply, I tell her, "I think the question is, what can *I* do for *you*?"

"Ah, you've been thinking about my offer." In my mind's eye she's wearing the same expression as a cat who's caught a canary in its mouth.

"I have," I tell her. "And I've realized that I don't have any reason to be loyal to Zach."

I'm shocked when she gives me a reason. "He's your boss's brother …"

"He is," I tell her. "And while I respect the heck out of Troy, I've never particularly thought highly of Zach."

"Have you met him before?" she wants to know.

Lifting my feet up onto the sofa, I take a sip of my coffee before answering, "No. But I've always been a big fan of yours and after seeing how he treated you, I don't see anything redeemable in him."

Once again, Yolanda surprises me. "Forgive me for having doubts, but yesterday it seemed you were on Zach's side."

Shoot, I thought she'd be so happy to hear from me that she wouldn't question that. "Yolanda," I say. "I would be lying if I didn't tell you that you come across differently in person than you do on television. I felt like I was on the receiving end of an attack."

"And you no longer feel that way?"

I'm going to have to be careful how I answer this. After a long pause, I say, "I spent all day and night thinking about things, and I realized that if I was in your shoes, I'd probably act the same way." I take a deep breath for courage before adding, "Men like Zachary Hart think they can do whatever they want and get away with it."

"And you could use twenty grand," she correctly surmises.

There's no point in lying to her about that. "Yes. But ultimately that's not the reason I'm helping you."

"Have you ever dated someone like Zach?" Yolanda wants to know.

"There aren't many Zachs in a town like Maple Falls. But I have dated guys I've really liked who had no interest in a long-term relationship, and it was humiliating. I can imagine how I'd feel if I were you and that happened in the public eye."

"It's devastating," Yolanda says. "Especially when the whole world is talking about it."

I highly doubt it's the whole world. In fact, nobody would be talking about it if she wasn't the one smearing Zach's reputation every chance she got.

I know Yolanda is a well-known figure, but I'm pretty sure she's overestimated people's interest in her private life. Of course, there's no way I'm going to tell her that. "Would you like to meet sometime today and discuss what you'd like me to do?"

My inquiry is met with silence, and I worry I might have somehow blown it. But then she says, "I've got to be at the rink later for the first press conference, so I'll be tied up with that. Then there's a bigger gathering at the Regent Hotel." I'm guessing the clicking noise I hear is her tapping a long fingernail against the phone. "How about if we meet tomorrow morning for breakfast up at the lodge?"

I'm a little surprised she's going to put it off that long, but I'm not about to push her. "Sounds good. How about nine o'clock?"

"I'll see you then." She hangs up before I can bring up the subject of money. Unfortunately, I'm no longer certain that working for Yolanda is the slam dunk I thought it would be. But then I remind myself that she's a reporter. As such, her instincts are likely going off like crazy. Which means I'm going to have to do my darndest so that I don't give her any reason to doubt me.

After drinking another cup of coffee, I eat breakfast and shower before getting dressed for the day. Then I call my mom.

The phone rings several times before a man answers. "Hello."

I'm caught off guard that it's not my mom, which causes me to stumble over my words. "Oh, hey ... um, hi ... is Elaine there? This is her daughter."

"This is Jake, Elaine's nurse. Your mom is having more tests done right now. She had a rough night, and the doctor wants to make sure she doesn't have a brain bleed."

Terror pours through my nervous system in an icy current. "A brain bleed?"

"As a result of her fall," he says. "The initial CT scan was done so soon after the accident, it wouldn't have shown a bleed unless it was extensive. But last night your mom was confused and agitated, so the doctor wants to rule out something worse than a concussion."

"I'm leaving the house right now," I tell him. "I'll be there in ten minutes."

"There's no point in hurrying," he says. "Your mom will be out of her room for a while yet. How about if I give you a call when she comes back?"

I realize that I need to be here when the hospital bed comes, so I tell him, "Okay, but please call as soon as she's back."

After hanging up, I start pacing around the room like I'm trying to wear a hole in the carpet. I should have asked Jake what it would mean if my mom had a brain bleed. How will they treat it? What are the repercussions of such a thing?

I'm about to start Googling it, when the front doorbell rings. I run to answer it, hoping it's Zach. I could really use a dose of his calming influence. But it's not him; it's the deliveryman with the bed.

"Come in," I tell him. "I'll show you where it's going."

Before he can comment, I lead him down the hall to my mom's room and point to the empty space in the center. "Right there."

As he nods his head, I notice the laugh lines around his eyes. If I had to put money on it, I'd say this guy is living a happy life. He hands me the clipboard he's holding. "I just need you to sign at the X on the bottom of the page." I quickly sign before handing the papers back.

"My partner and I will have this up and running in no time," he tells me before walking out of the room.

While I'm relieved to have a hospital bed for my mom, I worry that if she's really hurt herself, it might be too little, too late.

I force myself to go into the kitchen and wash dishes while the men get everything assembled. I tell myself things like, "Don't worry, Ellie, Mom is fine. She has to be fine." The problem is that I don't believe me. I've already lost my dad, so I know that bad things don't always happen to other people. The thought of living a life without both of my parents is more than I can bear right now.

I really want to run down to Zach's cottage and ask him to comfort me. Somehow, I know that if he told me everything was going to be all right, I'd be more inclined to believe it. Looking at the clock, I see that it's already after one, so I know that's not an option. By now, he's long gone to the arena for the first press conference of the day.

That's the thought that finally diverts me from my current worries. Zach and Yolanda are both at the rink and I can't help but wonder how that's going.

CHAPTER NINETEEN

Zach

Even though I took a two-hour nap on the hammock yesterday, I still slept like a baby last night. I haven't been this rested in years, which makes me think there's something about the air in Maple Falls that acts like a tranquilizer. Yet, I expect my sense of calm has more to do with Ellie than the air. She makes me feel peaceful and protective—even when she's grumbling at me, her presence is a balm.

Looking through my suitcase, I can't decide if I should wear a suit to the rink or if I should dress more casually. A suit might make me look like a stuffy billionaire—like I was trying to put myself above everyone else, and jeans could send the message that I'm not giving the event the amount of respect it deserves. I wind up splitting the difference and putting on a pair of khakis with a nice shirt, no tie.

I'm not usually the type of guy to overthink his wardrobe. The only reason I'm giving it any thought now is because of the damage Yolanda has done to my reputation. I want to see that woman today as much as I want to jump out of a plane without a parachute. Unfortunately, I have no doubt she's going to be at all the events and I'm going to have to keep my cool.

I'm tempted to stop and see Ellie on my way out today, but I think better of it after the way we parted company yesterday. While I thought we had a good day, she pulled back rather dramatically.

As soon as I get into the SUV, I turn on the ignition before rolling the windows down. Then I back out of the driveway and head toward my destiny. I hope Troy is right and this project will turn things around for me. Too bad when he created his plan, neither of us suspected Yolanda would be here.

As soon as I arrive at the arena, I run my fingers through my hair to tame the wind damage caused by the ride over here. After getting out of the car, I head toward the locker room. I assume all the players are here, but from the number of cars in the lot, it doesn't look like a ton of press have arrived. Most of them are probably going to skip it and just hit the main event later at the hotel.

Walking through the locker room door, I'm met by a scene that temporarily causes my throat to tighten. I see familiar faces I know from going to games over the years, like Noah Beaumont, a hotshot who was playing for a team out of New York until he bad boyed his way down to an AHL team. Troy always liked him, so I trust his judgment. But, hey, at least he got a shot at the NHL.

When I was injured in college, I had to force myself to put all things hockey behind me. It was an act of self-preservation. Yet standing amid so many players now—some that I know and some I don't—makes me feel a nostalgia that nearly brings me to my knees.

Even being on the ice with Tommy the other night didn't affect me like this. I'm about to turn and walk back outside when I hear a familiar voice. "Zach, my man! How the heck have you been?"

Turning around, I spy the familiar face of Dan Roberts—my nephew's hero. Sticking out my hand, I greet, "Dan, how are you? I hear you're the Ice Breakers captain."

Dan ignores my hand and pulls me into a man hug before proceeding to pat my back like he's trying to burp a gorilla. "Sure am," he says. "Happy to be back in Maple Falls."

Dan grew up here and talked about his hometown so fondly that when Troy was looking for a place to settle down, he decided he had to visit. He never left.

"I bet Maple Falls is happy to have you back."

Dan seems pensive for a beat before saying, "My family is."

Something about his tone makes me think there might be someone else who isn't as eager to see him. I'll have to remember to ask him about it at another time. I currently have bigger fish to fry. "Have you seen Troy?"

He points across the room. "He's in his office." Then he adds, "Watch out; I saw Yolanda Simms out there. That woman is bent on ending you, Zach."

"Tell me about it." I don't bother defending myself because I'm fairly certain Dan knows I'm not the kind of guy I'm being portrayed as being. "I'll see you later," I tell him before walking away.

I call out a few other greetings as I make my way across the room, but I don't stop moving until I'm standing at the entrance of the press room. Peeking through the small square window on the door, I see a dozen or so reporters, as well as my brother, who's shuffling through a stack of papers at a desk set up in front of the assemblage.

Troy looks up and sees me before standing up and joining me in the hall. "Hey, bro. You ready?"

"As I'll ever be, I suppose."

"Just play it cool," he tells me. "Yolanda is sure to ask questions about you and her, but I'll cut her off. Most of the folks inside are from local affiliates and not national ones, so I'm going to let them ask the bulk of the questions."

Nodding my head, I tell him, "Let's do this."

Before we meet the press, Troy crosses the hall and opens the locker room door. He shouts, "We're ready to start! Come on out into the hallway. I'll signal you when it's time to introduce you."

As soon as my brother and I walk into the press room, the reporters begin a barrage of questions. Troy raises his hand to quiet them before saying, "Welcome to the first annual Ice Breakers All-Star charity hockey tournament. I'd like to introduce you all to my little brother Zach."

"Oh, we know Zach," a man in the front calls out before asking, "What's going on with you and Yolanda?"

Instead of letting me answer, Troy says, "Zach is going to match all corporate donations of up to two million dollars."

"Is that because *The Tattler* accused you of being a tightwad, Zach?" a female reporter wants to know.

I shake my head before offering, "I donate a lot of money to charity, but I don't make all of those donations public. I'm participating in this event because I have a soft spot for kids in need."

"So you're not here to clear up your bad press?" someone else asks.

"I don't pander to anyone. Not even the press," I tell them.

"Not even when you've dumped one of us so unceremoniously?" Yolanda has entered the discussion.

"Yolanda," I say. "You and I went on three perfectly nice dates. I have no idea why you decided to announce to the world that we were in an exclusive relationship when we hadn't so much as held hands. My choosing not to see you after that cannot be called dumping you."

"Zach ..." She bats her eyes several times like she's trying to hold back tears. "I don't know why you're lying about us, but it really hurts."

"I don't know why *you're* lying," I tell her. "Not only is it unprofessional, but it makes you look like a fool." I didn't mean to add that last bit, but the woman has a way of riling me up.

"Do you always call your girlfriends fools?" This from the reporter who asked the first question.

"I don't call any of my girlfriends fools." I tell him. "Which should make it clear that Ms. Simms never held that title."

Before things can go more off the rails, Troy takes over. "I know a lot of you are hoping to get answers from my brother, but please remember that Zach and I are here to raise money for charity."

Troy spends the next half-hour introducing the players to the press, starting with local Maple Falls hero Dan Roberts. This has the desired effect of getting everyone back on task. While the team answers questions, I slip out of the room, hoping for a break from the chaos. Even though I shouldn't be, I'm surprised when Yolanda joins me.

"Are you ready to hear me out?" she asks.

I look at her sleek blonde hair and her overly made-up face and search for a clue as to why she's targeting me. "I have no desire to talk to you."

She rolls her eyes. "Zach, I have a proposition for you. If you'll just listen to me, you'll understand the genius of it."

"Does your proposition involve you telling the world that you're a liar?"

She scoffs loudly. "Of course not."

"Then I'm not interested." And even though I feel quite righteous in my indignation, a part of me can't help but wonder if I've just signed my own death warrant.

CHAPTER TWENTY

Ellie

I leave for the hospital as soon as the delivery men are done setting up my mom's bed. Regardless of what she says, I want to be there when she returns to her room.

After parking my car, I stop off in the cafeteria and get my mom a chocolate donut and myself an apple fritter. Then I take the elevator up to the second floor. The receptionist is a girl I went to high school with. "Hey, Jen. I'm here to see my mom."

She stands up and walks around the desk to give me a hug. "I was going to call you when I saw that Elaine was a patient. How is she doing? How are *you* doing?"

Ignoring the question about me, I tell her, "Mom had more tests this morning so I'm hoping for an update."

That's when a man wearing scrubs turns around and asks, "Are you Elaine's daughter?" I nod my head. "I'm her nurse, Jake. They just brought her back to her room, if you want to follow me."

I wave to Jen before hurrying after Jake. "Is she okay?" I ask him. "Is it a brain bleed?"

"I don't know," he says. "The doctor is still with her so you can ask him." He opens the door and leads the way.

My eyes immediately search out my mom. She's lying on the bed looking so small I almost don't believe it's her. "Mom." I approach her while asking, "How are you doing?"

She forces a pained smile. "I'm so tired, honey. All I want to do is sleep."

The doctor, who's on the other side of the bed, looks up at me from the chart in his hands. "I'm Ellie, Elaine's daughter," I tell him.

He nods his head once. "Your mom has a small hemorrhage in her brain due to her fall."

The panic I feel is nearly overwhelming. "Does that mean she'll need surgery?"

"I don't think so," he says reassuringly. "But we still want to monitor it for a couple more days."

"What if it doesn't stop?"

"Then we'll have to operate to alleviate the pressure. But from what I can see on the imaging, I'm optimistic the bleeding will stop on its own."

I have a million questions, but I don't want to worry my mom. Glancing at her, I see that her eyes are closed, so I quietly ask the doctor, "Is she going to be okay?"

"That's the plan."

"What can I do to help?"

"You can let her rest so her body will get to work healing itself."

"Okay," I tell him. "I'll just sit here with her."

My mom opens her eyes long enough to say, "Go home, Ellie. I'm fine."

"I'm not going to leave you here alone, Mom."

She closes her eyes again. "I'm not going to get better until you do."

"Mom …" I'm about to tell her that's a horrible thing to say. I need to be with her, if not for her sake, then for my own.

But before I can do so, the doctor interrupts. "Patients often feel stress from their loved ones, and it keeps them from resting. Go home and I promise someone will call you the minute your mom's situation changes."

Leaving goes against every instinct I have, but my mom's the one telling me to go. After several moments, I finally agree, "Fine, but I'm going to call in regularly."

"Not if I call you first," Jake says comfortingly. "I'll keep you updated on any changes."

Reluctantly, I lean down and kiss my mom on the cheek before heading toward the elevator. Luckily, Jen is chatting with someone else. I feel like I'm a breath away from bursting into tears and stopping to talk would definitely push me over the edge.

Walking out of the hospital feels wrong. It would be easier if I were teaching today or was expected at Kelly's, but I've got nothing. I'm going home to an empty house where I'll probably just sit and worry.

On the way home, I stop at the market and pick up ingredients to make homemade caramel. Candy making will force me to focus all my attention on the thermometer, so I don't burn it. Hopefully, that will be the perfect distraction.

After putting cream, corn syrup, and five pounds of sugar in my basket, I add Granny Smith apples and a bag of toasted chopped macadamia nuts. I only make caramel apples once a year and it looks like today is going to be that day.

I'm not surprised Zach's car isn't in the drive when I get home, but I'm still disappointed. I have no idea when he'll get back because he has a couple of press conferences and then a thing at the lodge with the team.

After unloading the groceries, I tie on an apron before pulling the stock pot out of the cabinet. I put it on the largest front burner before adding corn syrup, sugar, milk, and heavy cream. Then I start stirring it over a medium heat for what I know will feel like forever.

Yet today, the mixture almost hypnotizes me as it graduates from a pale ivory color to a thicker golden blend. When the candy thermometer hits two hundred and thirty-four degrees, I slowly add the remaining milk and cream and then repeat the stirring process until it reaches two hundred and forty-four degrees. Turning the flame off, I mix in the vanilla extract.

While the caramel cools slightly, I wash and dry the apples before laying them on a sheet of parchment on the counter. Then I pour the nuts into a bowl.

Looking at the clock, I realize a full hour has passed since I started, and I haven't worried about my mom once. *Ah, the power of homemade candy.* Unfortunately, once I have that realization, I start to fret again.

I find long wooden skewers in the pantry and insert them into the bottom of each apple. Once that task is completed, I take turns dipping the fruit into the caramel to cover the whole thing. When I pull them out, I gently twirl the stick to let the excess caramel fall off. Finally, I dip the apples into the chopped nuts before putting them back on the parchment to cool.

Once I'm finished with all twelve, I pour the remaining mixture into a small, buttered cake pan. I'll cut it and wrap it in individual portions after it cools completely. Turning my attention back to the finished product, I admire my handy work. It looks like a picture in a magazine.

I'm about to start cleaning up when my phone rings. I hurriedly pick it up. "Hello?"

"Ellie, it's Jake from the hospital."

A chill of dread starts at the base of my spine and rapidly shoots toward my head. "Is my mom okay?" I demand. "Is the bleeding worse?"

"Your mom is fine," he tells me. "I told you I'd call regularly, and I will until my shift ends at seven. I just wanted to let you know that you probably won't hear from the night nurse because your mom will be sleeping."

"Oh, okay," I tell him. "But she's good now?"

"She's great. She's resting."

"Do you work tomorrow?"

"I'll be back at seven in the morning," he says. "I'll ring you as soon as I get your mom's vitals." I thank him before hanging up.

After cleaning up the kitchen, I go into my mom's room and lie down on her new bed. I play with the remote, raising the mattress up and down like I'm a kid with a new toy. I can't wait to show her how easy it will be for her to get in and out of bed.

Somewhere along the line, I close my eyes and fall asleep for two whole hours, which is not something I normally do. I dream about Zach. I dream that he and I fall in love and get married before having enough boys to fill a hockey team of our own.

I'm not one to fantasize about outrageous things like marrying a billionaire, but now that Zach is in town and he's not the villain I thought he was, a part of me can't help but wonder if there's a fairytale ending to my story.

Looking at the clock, I discover it's already four thirty. I get out of my mom's bed and cross the room to the mirror to assess the damage to my hair. It's not as bad as it could be, yet I still run a brush through it and pinch my cheeks for color.

Walking down the hallway, I look out the picture window in the living room in hopes of discovering Zach's car. It's there, but being that I don't know how long he'll be home, I head to the kitchen and wrap a caramel apple for him in a sheet of cellophane. I tie the base with a raffia bow before walking down the path with my offering. The closer I get to Zach's cottage, the more excited I feel. It's freeing to not feel anger when I think about him. Yet, it's equally anxiety-inducing that I'm starting to feel something more.

I knock on his door but there's no answer, so I wait a few beats before repeating the action. Still, nothing. Why isn't he answering? I'd be lying if I said I wasn't a little worried, especially after what just happened with my mom. Turning the knob, I discover the door is unlocked so I walk in. "Zach?" I call loudly. "Where are you?"

Moments later, he comes running out into the living room with a towel haphazardly wrapped around his waist. "Ellie, are you okay? Is it your mom?"

I stare at him in what can only be described as complete awe. The man is an Adonis. "I … um ... fine …" My mouth dries up to the point where I can barely speak.

Zach hurries to my side and demands, "What's wrong?"

Shaking my head, I tell him, "Nothing. I … just …" I hold up the caramel apple between us, "brought you a treat."

Zach's eyes shift from concern to something else entirely. "A treat, huh?" The way he says that makes it clear he's not talking about the proffered apple.

My face heats up to the point where I'm pretty sure I'm about to spontaneously combust. Looking away, I tell him, "I made it myself."

"You made the caramel?" He sounds as impressed as he should. Making caramel isn't hard, but it is tedious.

"I did." I force myself to breathe so I don't wind up in a heap at his feet. There's only so much fainting—real or otherwise—I can do in his presence without looking like an invalid.

"What are you doing for dinner?" Zach suddenly asks.

"They're keeping my mom in the hospital for a couple more days so I'm on my own."

"Why don't I cook for us?" he asks. "It's the least I can do after you went to all the trouble of making dessert." Once again, I sense he's not talking about the apple and my face flushes hotly.

"What are you cooking?" I don't know why I bother asking because I'd say yes even if he were making mud pies.

"How about steak and potatoes? That's my specialty."

"You have to get dressed first," I say, sounding like a prissy schoolmarm out of the Old West.

Zach tightens the towel at his waist. With a smile, he says, "I'll be right back."

As soon as he leaves the room, I collapse onto the sofa in a heap. Holy cow, I just saw Zach without his clothes on and now he's going to cook for me. This is not what I expected when I came down here, but I'm sure as heck not going to complain.

Once again, I can't help but wonder if something might actually happen between me and Troy's hunky billionaire brother?

CHAPTER TWENTY-ONE

Zach

Even though I didn't come to Maple Falls looking for love, the more time I spend with Ellie, the more I wonder if there could be something between us. I know it would be prudent to keep my distance, but I can't help myself. I want to be with her.

My mind drifts toward Yolanda as I put on a pair of sweats and a T-shirt. She didn't make too much of a public scene today, which was surprising. Although she did make it clear the only reason she's in Washington is to make my life miserable.

Walking out of the bedroom, I ask Ellie, "Did you talk to Yolanda today?"

She looks me up and down, seemingly relieved that I'm no longer in my birthday suit—yet I choose to believe she enjoyed the view. "I talked to her this morning. We're having breakfast at the lodge tomorrow."

"Good. Make sure to ask for the money up front."

Ellie nods her head. "How did things go between you and her today?"

I sit down on the couch next to Ellie before answering, "Not great. I'm guessing it's going to get worse because once again I wouldn't hear her out."

"You really need to listen to her terms, Zach. You don't have to do anything about it if you don't want to."

"I don't want to give her the pleasure," I tell her. "If I listen to what she has to say, she's going to think she has the upper hand."

"Have you ever heard that old saying about not cutting off your nose to spite your face?"

"I've heard it," I tell her. "But there's another saying about not suffering fools lightly."

She laughs. "You're pig-headed, do you know that?"

Standing up, I tell her, "I just want to live my life by my rules."

"I think that's the definition of stubborn. My mom always says that if you don't learn to bend, then for sure you're going to break."

I walk into the kitchen, and I open a drawer before pulling out an apron and putting it on. "Let's see what you find out tomorrow," I tell her. "Maybe you'll be the answer to all my prayers, and I'll never have to bend." I try to sound lighthearted, but the truth is, Ellie's right. I'm stubborn and I like to get my way.

I take the steaks out of the refrigerator and put them on a dish before pouring Worcestershire sauce on them. Then I chop up a couple of garlic cloves and mix them with a little dijon mustard before rubbing the mixture onto the steaks.

"I have a bottle of wine up at the house if you're interested," Ellie offers.

I open the cupboard and pull out my favorite Cabernet. "I have one right here." Popping the cork, I pour her a glass and carry it over to her.

"It's not even five," she says, yet she still takes the glass.

Looking at my watch, I tell her, "It's seven fifty-eight in New York." Then I sit down next to her.

Exhaling loudly, she announces, "It's been a heck of a day." Then she takes a sip of her wine before declaring, "So good!"

I raise my glass in a toast. "Some days require a little help." I take a sip before asking, "Did your mom's bed arrive?"

"Oh, my gosh, Zach, it's so comfortable! I lay down on it and fell right to sleep."

"I hope you had sweet dreams," I croon. I shouldn't be flirting with Ellie, but I can't seem to help myself. She's so sweet and totally different from the women I usually date.

Is it me or does she blush while answering, "I had very nice dreams, thank you."

"You want to tell me about them?"

She shakes her head. "I don't think so."

The air in the room is suddenly so thick with tension that if I don't get some fresh air, I'm going to pull Ellie into my arms and kiss her the way I've been thinking about since we first met. "I'm going to grease the potatoes and then put them in the oven. Should we go for a walk while they cook?"

She looks so relieved by my suggestion, I wonder if she's been having similar thoughts about me. "That sounds like a great idea!"

Four minutes later, I put on a sweater and lead the way onto the front porch. "Have you always rented this place out?"

She shakes her head. "My dad built it for his mom. She lived here for ten years before she died."

My fingers twitch with the desire to reach over and take her hand in mine, but I don't. "You must have nice memories of that time."

"I really do," she says. "My mom's parents both died when I was little, so Nana Butler was all I had in the way of grandparents. She was a cool lady."

I walk toward the woods, thinking a brisk hike might be exactly what I need to push away the romantic thoughts I'm having about my landlady.

Ellie has other ideas. As soon as we near the hammock, she runs over and jumps onto it like a pro. "I like to come down here and stare up into the treetops like they hold all the answers to my problems."

She scoots over to make room for me, so I hesitantly sit down. "What are your problems?" Ellie doesn't answer, so I guess, "You're worried about your mom."

"All the time," she confesses. "Her arthritis has progressed so quickly, I'm afraid I'm going to have to put her into a facility. And that would kill her."

It would also cost a fortune, which I'm guessing is another of her concerns. "Try your mom on the turmeric when she gets home. It's amazing how many natural anti-inflammatories there are and how well they work."

"You'd think her doctors would have mentioned them."

Gravity is pulling both of us toward the center of the hammock and before you know it, Ellie is nearly on my lap. Valiantly trying to keep my mind off wrapping my arms around her, I announce, "Western medicine isn't known for being very open-minded about natural cures."

Ellie's body relaxes against mine. "My grandmother used to soak golden raisins in gin. She ate eight of them a day to help reduce the pain in her hands."

"Interesting." Her head is so close to mine that I can smell the floral scent of her shampoo. "Does your mom do that?"

"I'm not sure she even knew about it. But now that I've remembered, I'll pick up some raisins and gin so she can try it." She squirms like she's trying to get more comfortably situated, but with both of us on the hammock the only way to do that would be to lie down. And I'm not going to suggest that.

"If we're going to keep sitting on this thing," I tell her, "I'm going to need to put my arm around you." She tips her chin up to look me in the eye, which causes me to add, "Or I could just go sit on the ground."

Her response is so quiet I barely hear it. "You can put your arm around me." She leans forward which easily allows me to do so. Neither one of us says anything for the longest time. We just sit there, snuggled up together.

I can't remember the last time I felt so comfortable with a woman. Neither Ellie nor I seem to require conversation. We're just enjoying the peace, both lost in our thoughts.

Several minutes later, Ellie breaks the silence. "Tell me about your life in Los Angeles."

"It's very different from Maple Falls," I tell her. "It's go, go, go, all the time."

"That sounds awful," she says. "Do you have any place where you can just get away from it all?"

"I split my time between my condo in Beverly Hills and my beach house in Malibu. I'm most relaxed when I'm at the beach, but I still have a lot of neighbors."

"I love spending time at the coast," she says. "But I'd rather camp in the middle of nowhere than have other people right on top of me."

I want to tell Ellie she should come stay at my beach house sometime, but I don't want to scare her off. I don't want her to think I'm proposing something untoward. "How about if I lend you my house sometime when I'm not there? Maybe you and your mom could have a nice vacation together."

"Why when you're not there?" Is it me or does she sound hurt?

"I could be there, too," I say quickly.

"My mom doesn't like to travel anymore," Ellie announces, which effectively pops the balloon of excitement that had started to build at the thought of having her in my home. "It's too hard on her."

"Maybe she'll change her mind once she gets used to her wheelchair."

"Do you have wheelchair ramps?" she wants to know.

"Not yet, but I could get some."

"Zach." Ellie leans away from me so that she can turn her head and look at me. "You do not need to get wheelchair ramps for my mom."

"I don't *need* to do anything, Ellie. But I like to do things for my friends."

She smiles sadly before saying, "I could never reciprocate."

"You made me a caramel apple," I remind her.

She scoffs. "Yeah, but that was easy."

"And if you decided you want to visit my house in Malibu, it would be easy for me to have ramps installed."

Ellie's eyes narrow slightly before she says, "It's like we don't even live on the same planet."

While I know she's feeling a huge disparity in our lives, I feel the need to tell her, "It's a good thing that we have the capability to travel to other planets then."

"Maybe you and Elon Musk," she jokes.

"I think the kind of world-hopping I'm talking about can be done by anyone. Even you."

"I've never had a friend wealthy enough to have a beach house," she says.

"You do now," I tell her. Even if Ellie wants nothing more than friendship from me, I'll consider myself lucky. Although, I truly hope she wants more.

CHAPTER TWENTY-TWO

Ellie

Sitting on this hammock with Zach's arm around me is the most romantic thing that's happened to me in five years. How sad is that? Especially because I'm probably the only one with romance on the mind.

If I don't break the tension, I'm liable to beg him to run away with me. Which is why I announce, "It turns out my mom has a small brain bleed and they're going to keep her at the hospital for a couple of days."

"That's scary, huh?" After a beat he adds, "But I suppose it's better safe than sorry."

"They might have to operate if it gets worse."

Leaning against the hammock, Zach pulls me closer to his side. "We got her to the hospital early, Ellie. The doctors know what they're doing."

"Would you say that if it was your mom?" I ask.

He snorts. "Probably not. I'm just trying to keep you from worrying."

"I could use a distraction," I say before releasing an epic sigh.

Zach turns his head to look at me and his expression becomes serious. I start to worry, but then he says, "I have a distraction for you."

The intensity of his gaze causes chills to erupt all over my body. "What's that?"

His left eyebrow arches. "You may not be up for it."

"How will I know if you don't tell me what it is?"

"Ellie," Zach groans like he's in pain.

"Zach?"

"I would really like to kiss you, but I don't want you to get the wrong idea."

Holy crow, this is my Cinderella moment, sans the glass slipper. Although if he doesn't want me to get the wrong idea, he clearly doesn't want me to think it means anything. "You mean it's just a kiss and nothing more." And while the thought makes me a little sad, it doesn't in any way dampen my enthusiasm at the thought of a lip-lock with Mr. Hunky Pants.

Zach suddenly looks hurt. "No. *That* would be the wrong idea. I don't want you to take our kiss lightly." He hurries to amend his comment. "*If* you'll let me kiss you, that is."

I tip my head to the side like I'm in deep contemplation. I want him to kiss me, I just don't want to appear too easy. I finally decide, "I think a kiss would be okay, so long as you don't think that the money you're paying me to spy on Yolanda is the reason I'm doing it."

He looks appalled at the very idea. "I don't pay for kisses."

"In that case …" I lift my chin slightly for easier access.

Zach stares at me for several seconds before lowering his lips closer to mine. He moves so slowly I wonder if he's having second thoughts. I'm about to tell him he doesn't have to go through with it when our mouths finally connect.

If this was a cartoon version of us, fireworks would be exploding overhead, and hearts would be filling the air around us. My skin flushes with such heat it feels like I've just walked into an inferno. I have never felt this degree of sensation from the barest touch of a man's lips.

Leaning toward Zach, I moan his name before pressing my mouth more firmly against his. In response, he lifts me onto his lap and proceeds to devour me like I'm the most delicious thing he's ever tasted.

We remain wrapped around each other for another minute or a month—seriously, time has lost all meaning. All I know is that my body is full of the sweetest sensations that make me want to profess my undying devotion. Somehow, I force myself to keep quiet. I don't want to scare Zach away and I'd surely do that if I acted like a love-struck teenager.

Out of nowhere, I think of the offense he took when Yolanda declared them a couple after three dates. Zach and I haven't so much as been on one date. I don't think we can count today because our upcoming dinner was not planned, it was more a suggestion of convenience. Yet, this kiss … this kiss makes me wonder if we couldn't call today a date after all.

When Zach finally lifts his mouth from mine, all he says is, "Wow."

"Wow, that was great, or wow, I need lessons in how to kiss a man," I tease.

"If you got lessons, you'd kill me for sure." Leaning up, Zach gives me a quick peck before adding, "That was an amazing kiss."

"It was pretty good," I agree impishly.

"Pretty good? That's all you have to say about it?" Poor Zach, I've offended him.

I shrug my shoulders slightly. "I think I've forgotten it already. You might have to remind me."

Zach smiles slowly. "Forgotten, huh? Come here, woman." He wraps his arms around me even tighter before declaring, "I'm about to give you a kiss you'll never forget."

And just like that, we're once again connected. There's no tentative pressure this time. Instead, he kisses me like we have always belonged to each other and always will.

This new intimacy transports me right out of my skin to the point where I feel like I'm hovering in the atmosphere above myself. Yet even so, I'm conscious of the riot of sensations racing through my nervous system. It's like a million little explosions all over my body and I can't get enough of them.

"Zach ..." I murmur against his mouth. But he doesn't come up for air. Instead, he doubles down, claiming me for his own. I have never felt like this with another man, and I can never imagine anyone else creating this kind of chaos within me.

Zach doesn't release me when the kiss ends. Instead, he holds me closely against his heart and rests his chin on the top of my head. Then he asks, "Do you think you're going to forget that one?"

"Never," I tell him truthfully. "You can run off to the other side of the world and I will always remember this moment."

The thought of him leaving Maple Falls breaks my heart. But who am I to think that a man like Zach Hart would ever fall for a girl like me? Especially in such a short time. At some point he's going to leave Washington and I'll become nothing more than a distant memory. Which makes me wonder if I shouldn't just pull away from him and tell him we can never kiss again.

Zach breaks the silence. "A penny for your thoughts." I don't answer right away, so he says, "You're making me nervous, Ellie. I need to know what you're thinking."

I hesitate a moment before telling him, "I'm thinking that was the nicest kiss I've ever had."

He pushes me away so that I'm sitting up, my face hovering above his. "That kiss meant something. In fact, it meant a lot." It looks like I've offended him.

"If you say so."

"I do say so. What's going on here?" Now he sounds annoyed.

"You're only here for a short time and I live here. It's not like anything is going to happen between us."

"And that makes you sad?" He asks this in such a way that I have no other choice but to tell him the truth.

"Yes." I wait a beat before adding, "I feel sorry for the guy who comes after you, because there's no way he's ever going to be able to make me feel the things you do."

Zach's eyes narrow slightly. "Let's not talk about who comes next. I agree that I'm only in Maple Falls for a few weeks, but neither of us knows what will happen after that."

"Zach," I tell him. "I don't live my life just for me. I have a mother to take care of. I have to stay here to do that."

"I know what your obligations are. I'm simply suggesting that we take things one day at a time and don't overthink the outcome. Can you do that?"

"Theoretically, yes," I tell him.

"Theoretically?"

"I don't want to get hurt, Zach, but you kiss like a man who has the power to hurt me."

"If I have the power to hurt you, you have an equal ability to do the same to me."

"I didn't think of it like that." It's an intense thought to realize that Zach doesn't hold himself above me. That in the land of love, we're on equal footing.

"So, we'll take things one step at a time and see what happens?"

I nod my head slowly. "Okay."

And just like that, I wonder what I've agreed to. A few days ago, I hated the ground Zachary Hart walked on and now I'm giving him the ability to mess with my emotions. What in the world is happening here, and more importantly, why would I ever want it to stop?

CHAPTER TWENTY-THREE

Zach

Ellie Butler is a conundrum. She's fiery, self-assured, and determined, but at the same time she's sweet, vulnerable, and fragile. She's unlike any other woman I've been with before. In fact, she's unlike any other woman at all.

Most of the ladies I've dated have been driven to get what they want, whether that be the fame that comes with a connection to me or the kind of financial trappings they expect me to provide in a relationship. Even though Ellie has agreed to take my money, she's only doing so to help her mother. She's not looking to aid her own lifestyle. It makes me want to open my wallet and hand her the contents. Yet, I know she wouldn't take more than we've already agreed upon.

I understand her worry over what will happen between us when I leave, but there's no way of knowing. All we can do is live life in the moment. If something long-term is meant to be, it will be. And if not, I will be left with the sweetest memories of my lifetime.

"Our baked potatoes are probably done," I tell her. "Should we head back up to my cabin?"

She tries to gracefully stand up, but the nature of the hammock makes such a maneuver impossible. Wrapping my arm around her waist, I say, "Let's swing back and forth and on the count of three we'll stand up together."

While the plan seemed sound, it takes us four tries before we're finally free of the tree swing's gravitational pull. Ellie laughs loudly. "It's only a hammock for one so it's a miracle we got up at all."

While walking up the path hand in hand to my cabin, I can tell Ellie is still uncertain about our agreement to take things as they come. But I'm not going to let that bother me. I'm simply going to keep letting her know what a remarkable woman I think she is and how much I like her. Eventually, she'll have to believe me.

Opening the door, I let Ellie go in ahead of me. "It smells good in here," she says.

"Just wait until I get the steaks going. I'm going to broil them, if that's okay with you."

"I love steak no matter how it's cooked," she says before asking, "Do you have ingredients for a salad? I'm happy to put one together."

I point to the fridge. "I have enough fixings for an army."

We spend the next several minutes working alongside each other in the tiny kitchen. It feels intimate and domestic. Both of my kitchens, in Beverly Hills and Malibu, are big enough for entire hockey teams to easily work without getting in each other's way. But I like when my arm brushes against Ellie's. I like having her so close I can lean over and give her a peck on the lips whenever inspiration hits.

After pulling the steaks out of the oven, she asks, "Do you cook a lot at home?"

"Hardly ever," I tell her. "I eat out a lot and order take out. I find that I don't like to cook for one."

She gives me the briefest side eye. "Don't you ever cook for anyone else?" Her meaning is clear. She wants to know if I cook for other women.

"I occasionally cook for Belle, but only when she stays late."

Ellie drops a tomato onto the counter so hard it spurts juice. "Who's Belle?" Her tone is laden with jealousy.

I like knowing that I mean enough to her to incite the green-eyed monster, even if she doesn't want me to know it. So instead of answering her straight out, I ask, "Haven't I mentioned Belle?"

"You have not." She's practically leaning all her weight onto the tomato now and I don't see how we're going to save it.

"Belle is my assistant," I tell her. "She's my right hand, my drill sergeant, and my sentry at the gate. I'd be lost without her."

Ellie's expression slowly shifts from anger to relief. "She isn't by any chance eighty, is she?"

Shaking my head, I tell her, "Belle is in her early thirties and she's quite lovely. But before you get the wrong idea, she has no interest in me beyond the paycheck I give her, and the occasional perks that come from being my assistant."

Ellie's eyebrows furrow deeply. "What kind of perks?"

"Belle lives in Pasadena and often remarks how horrible the commute is, so I told her she could move into my condo while I was in Maple Falls."

"And when you go back?" Ellie's suspicion is adorable.

"If she hasn't donated all my stuff and redecorated to suit her own style, then she'll move back to Pasadena. If she's claimed the place for her own," I tease, "I'll have to buy myself something else."

I can't tell what Ellie's thinking because she suddenly gets very quiet. I watch as she cuts a cucumber and a red onion and tosses them into the salad. She even picks up the decimated tomato and breaks it apart into the bowl. I am determined to understand what's going on in her head, so I ask, "What are your thoughts?"

Looking up at me, she answers, "I can't put them into words. I mean, I've never known anyone like you before, so I don't know if you're teasing or if you'd actually give your assistant a condo and buy another. All I know is that we really do live in different worlds."

"Ellie, what would you do if you won the lottery?"

She thinks for a minute before asking, "How much would I be winning in this scenario?"

"For the sake of conversation, let's say forty-seven billion, give or take."

Her eyes pop open so wide they look like they're in jeopardy of falling out of her head. "Forty-seven billion *dollars*?"

"Dollars, coconuts, whatever currency you want."

She exhales loudly. "If she's as good of an assistant as you say, I'd let her keep the place."

I press a finger onto the steaks to make sure they're at the right temperature. "Then you think I'd be doing the right thing."

"I guess. I mean, maybe. I mean, how the heck do I know? There is a zero percent chance I'm going to win forty-seven billion dollars in the lotto. I don't even play."

Pulling two plates out of the cabinet above our heads, I serve the steaks and potatoes before saying, "Why don't you bring the bowl over to the table?"

I lead the way and when we're both seated, Ellie reaches out and picks up a lighter sitting next to the candles. "My parents always used to eat by candlelight. My dad said that it made even the simplest meal special."

"I agree with your dad," I tell her. "Belle got it into her head to replace all my wax candles with high-end battery-operated ones that automatically turn on every night at five and then turn off at eleven. I think it's kind of freaky."

Putting her napkin in her lap, Ellie says, "There are really good fake candles these days."

"Do you use them?"

She shakes her head. "No, but only because I like to watch the flame jump around. I also like the way the smoke smells when I blow them out."

After refilling our wine glasses, I lift mine and toast, "To real fire."

She adds, "That can burn you if you're not careful."

We're clearly not talking about candles anymore. "Real risk is part of finding a real connection."

Ellie gently taps her glass to mine. "To risk."

"To connection," I repeat.

We proceed to eat our meal slowly with the bare minimum of conversation. Silence isn't awkward with Ellie. It's comfortable and contemplative. I know she has a lot on her mind, and I certainly have a lot on mine.

When we're done eating, I pick up our dishes and carry them to the sink. Then I ask, "Would you like me to build a fire? We can sit on the couch and watch the flames together."

She's silent for so long I start to get nervous that she's going to say no. But she finally answers, "I'd like that, Zach. Why don't you get it ready while I cut up the caramel apple?"

Relief pours through me. What I'm feeling for Ellie is not some fleeting thing. She's the same kind of woman as my mom and Kelly. She's the kind of woman you build a life with, the kind you want to take care of and make happy for as long as you live.

While that realization should scare me to death, especially as we just met, I'm old enough to know a prize when I see one. I'm also smart enough not to let such a lady get away.

CHAPTER TWENTY-FOUR

Ellie

I roll over in bed and proceed to relive every moment of last night. Zach is nothing like the man I expected him to be. Yes, he's richer than any one person needs to be, and he's as handsome as an old-school movie star, but he's also kind and generous. Not only did he help me get my mom to the hospital, but he's making sure I have the funds to make her life more comfortable.

After our dinner, I wanted to spend the rest of the night wrapped in Zach's arms. I could have kissed that man for days on end, but that's not what we did. We spent time talking about ourselves and getting to know what makes each other tick.

For instance, I told him I would rather live simply if it meant I could help others. He told me that he donates the bulk of his charitable contributions anonymously because giving should be done out of true generosity and not for societal credit.

"Even though some people think you're stingy because of it?" I asked.

He explained that while he cares how he's portrayed in the press, doing the right thing matters more. Zachary Hart is most definitely the kind of man I see myself having a future with and that scares me.

After walking me up the path to my house, he gave me another toe-curling kiss goodnight. Then he waited until I'd gone inside and turned on the lights before leaving. I know this because I peeked out the window and watched him go.

My phone alarm jolts me out of my reverie and alerts me that I only have thirty minutes to get up and get ready for my breakfast with Yolanda. I'm curious to hear what she has to say about her "relationship" with Zach. Especially because before I knew him, I was ready to believe every word out of her mouth.

Jumping out of bed, I hurry to put on a pair of jeans and a sweater before brushing my hair and pulling it back into a pony-tail. I'm neither trying to impress Yolanda, nor compete with her, so the only makeup I bother with is lipstick.

I think about Zach the whole drive up to the lodge. I fantasize that we fall in love, and he moves to Maple Falls. I imagine us raising a family alongside Troy and Kelly's. My favorite visual is of walking our kids to the same elementary school that I went to. I'm not normally prone to such flights of fancy, but Zach is like no other man I've ever gone out with. As presumptuous as it sounds, I'm starting to feel he could be my forever.

The parking lot at the lodge is full of more cars than I've ever seen here. There are news vans, big black SUVs, and even a couple of limousines out front. Look out, Maple Falls, we're about to see the most excitement our town has ever experienced.

I hurry to go inside and discover the lobby is buzzing with activity. I suddenly wish I'd made more of an effort to look nice. When I get to the dining room, I give the hostess my name and tell her who I'm meeting.

She leads the way to a table right next to the vaulted window overlooking the river. Yolanda is talking on the phone and only offers the briefest nod of recognition that I've arrived. Sitting down across from her, I do my best to look relaxed, but the whole time I'm studying her like she's a lab rat.

Yolanda Simms is polished in a way that only money can provide. I've never colored my hair, but I'm guessing by all the highlights running through Yolanda's hair, she spends a fortune to achieve its intricate weave of tones. She's wearing eyelash extensions that are a touch too long but I know look good on television. She also has on a lot of makeup, but again, probably so that she's camera ready.

I'm about to dissect her manicure—are those acrylics or the result of long-time gel polish?—when she hangs up and says, "Ellie, I'm so happy you could make it."

"I'm happy to be here," I lie. I no longer believe Yolanda is telling the truth about Zach, but I still have to do my best to appear like I'm on her side.

She takes a sip of water before saying, "So, you've decided to help me."

I figure the truth is the best way to proceed. "My mom has some health needs, and I could use the money."

She nods her head slowly. "And what about Zach? What do you think about him?"

"Like I told you the other day, I don't know him."

"But you work for his brother," she prompts.

I exhale slowly before telling her, "Troy Hart is a great guy. Not only does he do a lot of charity work, but he's a wonderful family man. From what I can tell, his brother is nothing like him."

Yolanda surprises me by bursting into tears, and she's no delicate crier. After several moments of near hysteria, she finally settles down. "Zach is a wonderful man. We had three amazing days and nights together. I really thought we were destined for the long haul."

Either Yolanda is one heck of an actress or Zach did not tell me the truth about what went on between them. "If that's true, then why is he telling everyone you were never a couple?"

She loudly blows her nose into a napkin before answering, "Zach has been hunted by a lot of women who see him as a means to an end."

I remember what Zach said about Yolanda wanting to be seen with him so she could get her own national talk show. "But not you?"

Yolanda shakes her head. "I'm successful in my own right. I make a lot of money, and I don't need Zach for anything other than …" She leans toward the center of the table before lowering her head like she's about to confess to murder. "I'm going to need you to sign a non-disclosure agreement about what I'm about to tell you."

This is my chance to make sure she agrees to pay me in cash, so I tell her, "I'm happy to, after you pay me." My face flushes by how mercenary that sounds, so I add, "I would prefer being paid in cash so I can start paying my mom's medical bills. She's in the hospital right now."

Yolanda doesn't appear shocked by my request—almost like she's paid a bribe or two before. "What's your PayPal handle?" I write it on a napkin and slide it over to her as she picks up her phone. She hits several buttons before declaring, "Sent." Then she puts her phone down and refocuses her attention onto me.

As soon as my phone pings, I pick it up and discover that Yolanda did indeed transfer the money. I'd no sooner be able to initiate a transaction like that than I would be able to fly to the moon by simply flapping my arms. "What is it you need Zach for?"

Once again, tears pool in the reporter's eyes. "I need him to give our child his last name."

I don't know what I was expecting her to say, but it was not that. "Excuse me?!" I didn't mean to yell that, but I cannot believe what she just said.

Yolanda looks from side to side to see how many people are staring at us. Luckily, with all the famous hockey players around, my outburst didn't create much of a scene. "Zach and I slept together for the first time on our first date." Cue the tears to start falling harder.

It's not that I find it hard to believe Yolanda would sleep with someone on the first date, but Zach made no move to do more than kiss me last night. Could that be because he doesn't find me as attractive as Yolanda? My heart sinks as doubt circulates through me.

Yolanda doesn't appear to notice my turmoil. Instead, she sighs dramatically and says, "That man could kiss the spots off a leopard." The little hairs all over my body shoot straight up in response. Even though I agree with her, how would she know that unless she's been kissed by Zach—which is something *he* claims never happened.

"So, you slept with him on your first date ..." I know I sound judgy, but I don't care. I'm madder than a wet hornet. I *believed* everything Zach told me.

Yolanda's left eyebrow lifts toward her hairline. "I'm not embarrassed that I did. I'm just mortified he won't be truthful about it." She moves her hands around herself like she's spokes-modeling a microwave on *The Price is Right*. "What man in his right mind wouldn't want the world to know he'd been with me?"

"I ... um ... that is ..." I'm in awe of any woman who has this kind of innate confidence about herself. Even though I'm reason-ably attractive, I'm not cocky about it.

Yolanda continues, "I'm about to be visibly pregnant and the father of my child is going out of his way to make me look like I'm a crazy stalker."

"Don't take this the wrong way," I tell her. "But you're the one raking him through the coals in the press."

Her posture jerks upright. "Are you taking his side over mine?"

I obviously don't want her to think that, especially because I'm no longer sure who's telling the truth. "I'm just playing the devil's advocate," I tell her. "But you're the one giving the interviews."

Her nostrils flare slightly. "In the first interview I simply said that Zach and I were in a committed relationship. Nothing more."

"The following week, you told Whoopi Goldberg he was a misogynist pig," I remind her.

Yolanda slams her water glass down, sending icy drops flying in my direction. "Because he claimed I was nothing to him! I'm growing the man's child, Ellie." She starts crying again, and darn if she isn't portraying a sympathetic character.

"Does Zach know you're having his baby?" My throat tightens as the word "baby" comes out. It sounds like I'm gasping for my final breath on earth.

"No, but he'll say it's not his when he finds out."

"And you say otherwise."

Her left eye narrows like she's activating a death ray. "Zach is the only man I've slept with in the last six months. I'm only two months pregnant. You do the math."

I'm so off kilter right now, I don't know what to think. The only reason I'm starting to believe Yolanda is because she knows what a great kisser Zach is—*and he is*. He, on the other hand, is claiming they never kissed. How would Yolanda have this information about him if she wasn't telling the truth?

"I suppose you could get a DNA test," I tell her.

"That's a given." She says this with such certainty I feel a stab of pain in my heart. If Yolanda is *that* sure Zach will be confirmed as the father, then he likely is. My skin burns hot with betrayal. I can't believe he lied to me about this. Worse yet, I can't believe I changed my mind about him and believed he was telling the truth when he told me Yolanda was making everything up.

If what she says is true—and I'm now realizing it probably is—then the only reason Zach kissed me last night was to ensure I'd be on his side when I met with Yolanda. Why else would the man agree to give me forty thousand dollars unless he was trying to buy my loyalty? I suddenly feel hollow, like I've been drained of all my strength.

My phone pings, and I look down and read the incoming text.

MR. WONDERFUL

Good morning, beautiful. I can't stop thinking
about last night.

I look at the message with distaste. What a cheesy line, and one
Zach probably uses a lot. Looking across the table at Yolanda, I
ask, "What do you want me to do?"

"I want you to find out whatever you can about Zach from his
brother, his brother's wife, or him directly if you have any contact
with him." She eyes me closely. "You said at the rink that you'd
only just met him, but there was something that made me think
there might be more to it than that."

This is my big moment to pick a side. Do I think that Zach
could be Yolanda's baby daddy? *Yes.* Do I believe he's using me
for some nefarious purpose of his own design? If he's the father,
then I have to. Why else would he make a play for a nobody small
town girl he had nothing in common with?

"Yolanda," I tell her. "Would it help if I told you where Zach is
staying while he's here in Maple Falls?"

"Isn't he at his brother's?" she asks. "I just assumed that was
the case when I found out he wasn't here or at the other hotel in
town."

Without hesitation, I announce, "He's staying in a guest
cottage at the back of my mom's property."

Yolanda's gaze narrows perceptibly. "Are you sure there's
nothing going on between the two of you?"

I shake my head, pushing all thoughts of Zachary Hart's knee-
buckling kisses out of my mind. I force myself not to think about
those sexy green eyes of his and I certainly ignore the memory of
that soaking wet T-shirt he wore while washing windows.

"He's nothing more to me than a short-term tenant," I tell her.
And even though that's the truth, it still hurts a heck of a lot more
than it should.

"Good," Yolanda says. "Because I have a plan."

CHAPTER TWENTY-FIVE

Zach

I'm surprised Ellie hasn't texted me back, but then I remember she's at the lodge having breakfast with my nemesis. I know Yolanda will do her best to get Ellie to turn against me, but after the wonderful time we had last night, I hope she stays firm in her belief that I'm telling the truth.

After pouring myself a cup of coffee from the breakfast station, I peruse the buffet of offerings. I grab a blueberry muffin before sitting down in the stands and watching the team warm up.

Ever since my skating career ended, I've done my best to stay far away from all things hockey. Not because I've lost my love for the game, but to protect myself from my past dream resurrecting against my will.

The guys are a hoot to watch. Some players like Dan and Dawson already know each other from playing on the same team, while others have a natural competitive vibe due to playing on opposing NHL teams. The newer guys particularly seem to be out for blood until Coach Strickland hollers, "No cheap shots! You knuckleheads are on the same team now."

I feel a pull toward the ice in the worst way. After Ellie made me put on skates the other night, I thought I could handle being so close to the game, but that doesn't seem to be the case. While ice skating with a two-year-old is technically still skating, it's about as similar to hockey as dancing on the moon.

Troy glides over toward me. "You want to be out here, don't you?"

"Obviously," I tell him. "But unlike you, I can't just play around without breaking teeth."

Ignoring my cranky jab, my brother says, "You were a great player, Zach. It sucks that you got benched."

"Don't placate me," I hiss.

He laughs. "Quit being such a baby and get out here so we can get some pictures for the press."

Standing up slowly, I tell him, "I'll walk around and stand behind the team. I'm not going onto the ice."

"You came out the other night."

"I'm not in the mood to argue with you, Troy. You either want me in the pictures or you don't." I don't have to remind him that the only reason I'm here is to make sure there's a lot of press coverage for his event.

My brother rolls his eyes. "Someone woke up on the wrong side of the bed." Then he points toward the goal. "Meet us over there."

My phone rings as he skates away. Hoping it's Ellie, I don't bother checking caller ID before answering. "Good morning."

"Zach, it's Anthony Jenkins, from Fame."

Shoot. "Hey Tony, what's up?"

"I hoped I would have heard from you by now. Did you get the message I left with your assistant?"

"I did. I'm sorry I haven't had a chance to return your call." The truth is I've been so annoyed by the way Fame has been handling the situation with Yolanda, that in my head, we've already parted ways.

"I wanted to let you know that we've decided to cut ties with

Yolanda," he says. "We've learned some things about her that we find concerning."

"Oh? What have you learned?" *Maybe that she's a lying she-wolf bent on world domination?*

He clears his throat loudly before saying, "According to her agent, the stakes have been raised for her to get her own show. It used to be any semi-attractive person with vocal cords could be a talk show host, but nowadays the slots are rare."

"We all knew she wanted her own show and was willing to go to whatever lengths necessary to get it. What's changed?"

"All we knew was that she needed to be able to secure big names," Tony says. "But now she's looking to create a major scandal."

I roll my eyes. "Isn't that what she's been doing all this time?"

"There's more to it than that."

I stop my progression toward the team and lean against the boards. "Is she telling everyone I'm an alien come to Earth to prepare it for takeover?" Sarcasm drips from my words.

"She's pregnant."

My knees nearly buckle. "Excuse me?"

"We have a confidential source who works at a fertility clinic in Beverly Hills. A lot of our clients who don't want the world to know they're having trouble conceiving use them."

"And?"

"Yolanda had an IVF transfer two weeks before her first date with you."

I feel simultaneously feverishly hot and icy cold. It's like my nervous system can't keep up and all pistons have decided to fire at once. "She had in vitro right before our first date." I'm hoping that by repeating him, my brain will absorb the information.

"Which can only mean one thing," Tony says.

"She's been planning to pin a baby on me since the start of this charade."

"Exactly."

"While that's horrific," I tell him, "All it will take is a DNA test to show I'm not the father."

"That's old school thinking, Zach."

"How do you figure? If I'm not the dad, I'm not the dad. End of story."

"Don't you remember the Sharman Feliz case from two years ago?"

"I'm a busy man, Tony. I don't hang around the house watching Court TV." I know Tony isn't the bad guy here, but it's hard not to sound annoyed, especially as his firm has done nothing to help me out until now.

"Sharman was the woman who accused the Spokane Snow's goalie Hondo Hudson of getting her pregnant."

"The world is full of opportunists, Tony." I say this knowing he's already fully aware of that. Heck, he's probably representing half of them.

"True, but while the DNA test showed Hondo wasn't the father, Sharman had a slew of supporters who claimed he paid off the doctor to say it wasn't him."

I exhale loudly. "He doesn't have to pay her child support, so what's the problem?"

"He may not have to pay child support, but he *is* paying. He's lost all his corporate sponsors, and the Snow is trading him down."

"So, you're saying the truth doesn't matter and all a person needs to damn another is the right kind of press?"

"Or the wrong kind of press. And being that Yolanda *is* press, she can spin this story any way she wants."

I run a hand roughly through my hair. "Has she told anyone about the pregnancy?"

"Not yet."

"But she obviously will."

Tony says, "We think she's going to do it while she's up there in Maple Falls, where she's got you both figuratively and literally cornered."

"What if I came back to California?"

"She'd use it to her benefit to tell the world that as soon as you found out about the baby, you ran."

I start pacing back and forth like a caged bear. "What if I leave before she tells anyone? If I come back now, it'll be her word against mine that I know anything."

Tony is quiet for a beat before saying, "She's already got public opinion on her side." He's quiet for a minute before adding, "Come back today and don't tell anyone you're leaving."

"I've got to tell my brother. But other than him, I won't say a word."

"Don't tell *anyone*, Zach. I'm going to talk to Yolanda and see if I can guide her into announcing this while she thinks you're still there in Maple Falls."

Now I'm confused. "I thought you said you were canceling her contract?"

"Yolanda doesn't know that yet. And while PR people are notoriously hired to clean up unsavory messes, I don't like my firm being associated with creating them."

I think about Ellie again and wonder what Yolanda is telling her. I'm seriously starting to get nervous that she hasn't returned my text. "So, you're going to play both sides?"

"Yes, but the only way it will work is if you drive to the airport and get on your plane and come home without telling anyone."

It feels wrong to leave town without giving Ellie or Troy a heads up, but Tony might be the only person I know who can turn this storm around before it decimates my life.

"I have team pictures and a couple of interviews, but I'll leave for the airport right after that. I'll be in LA by this afternoon." I quickly text my pilot to let her know that I need her.

Tony says, "Go to your beach house and hole up there. I'll be in touch tonight."

I have to trust that between me and Yolanda, I'm the person Tony wants to keep happy. If there's one thing you can count on in Hollywood, it's that people always like to back the winner. As disgusting as it sounds, being that I have the most money, I'm the perceived winner in this dog race.

CHAPTER TWENTY-SIX

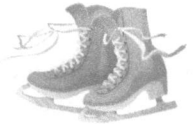

Ellie

I don't know whether to trust Yolanda or Zach. I believed Zach last night, but that was before I found out Yolanda was pregnant. And even though she could be lying about that, she went on and on about what a great kisser Zach is. Since he said he never kissed her, that makes him a liar. And if he'd lie about something as small as a kiss, it stands to reason he'd lie about something bigger —like sleeping with her. The whole thing disgusts me.

The only thing I know for certain is that someone isn't being honest, and I'm somehow smack in the middle of it. Of course, that's my fault for accepting money from both of them. I vow to return the money to whomever is telling the truth—once I know who that is. It's the only way I'll be able to live with myself for having anything to do with these people.

After I left the lodge, I drove over to the hospital to see my mom. I've been sitting in her room waiting for her to wake up for that last hour, but she hasn't budged. The doctor said he upped her pain meds, and I know the effect that has on her.

My mom doesn't stir until I've been sitting here for over two hours. Her first words are, "I thought I told you to stay away."

"Hello to you too," I say while reminding myself that a grouchy Mom is better than an unconscious one.

"I'm sorry," she grumbles. "I just hate being here. I want to be home and sleep in my own bed."

I wonder if I should tell her that her bed no longer exists, but I decide to hold off. "Any news from the doctor?"

She shakes her head slowly. "I don't go back for another scan until the day after tomorrow. They want me to just lie here and get as much rest as I can. You know how much I hate that."

My mom does not like being immobile, and she particularly dislikes that the pain meds make her so groggy.

"Maple Fest is less than a week away," I tell her. "What do you say we go this year?"

"How am I going to be able to manage all the steps needed to enjoy the festival? I can barely walk across the room."

"I rented you a wheelchair," I tell her.

Given her current mood, I expect her to be mad, but she's not. Instead, she looks almost relieved. "You did?"

"I've decided it's time to get you out among the living again and the only way that's going to happen is if you have wheels."

Tears fill her eyes. "Thank you, Ellie. I know I haven't been easy to live with, but you are always there for me. You're always thinking about things that will make my life easier."

I walk over to the side of her bed and take her hand. "I want you to start enjoying your life again. I'm also looking into some alternative treatments that I hope will help with your inflammation."

"I'd like to go to the arena with you sometime and watch your lessons," she says. "I feel like I haven't supported you nearly as much as you've supported me."

"You're welcome to join me anytime," I tell her. "Although, our schedule is a bit off due to Ice Breakers' practices."

Mom pushes the button on her bedside remote until she's in a sitting position. "I love that Troy and his brother are raising

money for Happy Horizons. Children are the world's responsibil-
ity, and we owe it to the future of humanity to take care of *all* of
them, especially the ones who aren't lucky enough to be born with
a leg up."

Zach is not my favorite person right now, so I agree, "Troy
really is a good guy."

"That Zach sure is cute." My mom's insinuation is as subtle as
a sledgehammer. She wants me and Zach to get together—which
can no longer happen.

"I suppose he's okay …"

"Just okay? Are you blind, girl?"

"He's a rich playboy, Mom. I'm not about to become one of his
groupies." I don't mention that last night I was ready to sign on as
president of his fan club.

"You are a lovely girl, Ellie. You're talented, and sweet, and
hardworking. You deserve happiness as much as anyone, and if
that comes in the form of a gorgeous billionaire, I say jump on
that horse."

I sit down on the edge of her bed. "Word on the street is that
he's not that nice to the women he dates."

"If you're talking about Yolanda Simms, I wouldn't trust that
woman as far as I could throw her."

"Why is that?"

"Don't you remember the big scandal she was involved in a
few years back? She dated that married film producer. The guy
left his wife and kids for her and then she broke it off with him to
chase after somebody else."

"I remember something, but not details," I tell her. There's so
much scandal attached to fame, it's hard to stay on top of it all. "I
thought the guy left her."

"Who cares who left who; she was fooling around with a
married man. That says something about the woman's character."

"It says something about the man's character, too," I remind
her. "After all, he was the one who made marriage vows."

"Agreed. I'm just saying that I'd be careful believing something you know nothing about."

She makes a good point. If Yolanda was in another dating scandal like my mom remembers, that should be enough to make me question her integrity. After all, unscrupulous women have lied about pregnancy since the dawn of time. I'm a little embarrassed at how quickly I jumped on the Zach-is-a-cad bandwagon. I guess I was trying to sabotage us or something.

Is it possible that I don't believe Zach because I don't think I deserve a great guy like him? In my wildest imagination, I couldn't have conceived someone of his status taking interest in me. I always saw myself dating a plumber or lumberjack—you know, a guy with a normal job. Billionaire men are not in my wheelhouse. I hate feeling all over the place like this.

I suddenly remember that I told Yolanda where Zach was staying. Shoot, why did I do that? "Mom," I say. "I'm going to go make a quick call. I'll be right back."

"You can make the call here."

"I'm going to get a soda out of the vending machine, too," I tell her. "Do you want anything?"

"I'll take a cola if you're offering." She smiles like a kid about to get a candy bar. My mom loves soda more than anyone I know. She says the carbonation feels like little fireworks on her tongue.

"I'll be right back." I grab my purse and leave the room. Once I'm in the hall, I pull out my phone and call Zach. There's no answer, so I leave the following message: "Hey, Zach, it's Ellie. I've been at the hospital with my mom. Call me when you get a chance."

As I put dollar bills into the vending machine, I worry what Yolanda is going to do with the information about Zach staying in my mom's cabin. She can't walk onto the property without my knowing it, but still, the last thing my mom and I need is a media circus in our own backyard.

Taking the sodas back into my mom's room, I discover she's fallen asleep again. I leave the cola on her nightstand, and I write a quick note that I'll check in later. Then I hightail it back home in case Yolanda shows up.

I really hope Zach calls me back soon. Even though I'm still back and forth about who to believe, I feel like a conversation would help me find my equilibrium.

CHAPTER TWENTY-SEVEN

Zach

While flying to Los Angeles, I try to figure out what plan Tony might have that will show Yolanda for the scheming woman she is. I come up dry. All I can think about is that Yolanda had to have set her sights on me long before we went out for the first time. The whole thing makes my skin crawl.

By the time I land in Santa Monica, I want to find the first reporter I can and share Yolanda's plot with the world. Yet if I do that, she can still spin it like I'm a crazy man bent on destroying her. And let's face it, there's no one more sympathetic than a single pregnant woman who claims the father of her child wants nothing to do with her—especially if that guy is a well-known billionaire.

Instead of calling an Uber to pick me up, I ask my pilot, Jenny, to give me a ride. Jenny has been with me for five years and she's proven to be as tight-lipped as they come. I've had some big celebrities and politicians on my plane, and she acts like they're no more special than her daughter's soccer buddies.

When we get into her Toyota, she asks, "Will we be flying again anytime soon?"

"You got big plans?" I ask. I usually give Jenny two days' notice before I need to leave but sometimes, like today, I need her on the spur of the moment.

"Hallie wants to have a sleepover with her friends this weekend and Al wants no part of it." Al is Jenny's ex and he's not the biggest help when it comes to raising their daughter.

"I honestly don't know, Jen. Something big is about to happen and my schedule is at the mercy of how things go down."

"No worries," she says. "Honestly, I want four eleven-year-olds sleeping at my house about as much as I want to get married again." She clarifies, "Which is never."

"Tell Hallie I'll make it up to her. I'll even get her and her friends tickets to the next Taylor Swift show if she wants."

Pulling out of the airport, Jenny tells me, "No way. You are not going to spoil my daughter. Her dad tries to buy her affection enough in place of spending time with her. I will not have her thinking men are there just to heap gifts on her."

"You're a good mom, Jenny."

"It's not easy." She sounds like she has the weight of the world on her shoulders.

I remember my mom saying that being a parent was like walking on water in the middle of a hurricane. And that was with my dad right at her side. I cannot imagine how difficult being a single parent is, especially when you have to balance an ever-changing work schedule.

"I could give you the tickets instead," I tell Jenny.

She scoffs. "You can't tempt me with concert tickets, Zach. However, if a gift certificate to Burke Williams showed up in my purse, I wouldn't complain."

"For a two-hour massage?" I guess.

"Make that a four-hour massage and a facial." The look on her face says she's teasing, but I know she could use the break. I quickly text Belle and ask her to make a call and help me make Jenny's dreams come true.

The traffic on Pacific Coast Highway is a nightmare, so I spend the time answering emails. By the time we turn into The Colony, the exclusive gated community where I live, I'm nearly caught up on my correspondence.

Rolling down her window, Jenny shows her ID to the guard at the gate and then proceeds down the road to my house. As she pulls into my driveway, she asks, "Do you need anything else?"

"Just your normal discretion," I tell her. "If anyone asks, I'm not here."

I wave to Jenny as she drives off before I go inside. I nearly scream like a little girl when I see my twin, Mac, standing in my living room. "Holy crap, man, what are you doing here?"

He appears as surprised as I am. "I called your assistant and said that I needed to talk to you. You didn't call back."

"I didn't have time," I tell him. "I've been busy trying to put out a fire."

"Firestorm Yolanda?" he asks.

I walk through the living room and out onto the deck. Mac follows. "Yolanda is pregnant," I tell my brother before sitting down on a reclining chair.

"With your kid?" His horror is apparent.

"That would be physically impossible. But she's going to tell the world it's mine."

He sits down next to me. "Yours or not, that's gonna make you look bad. You'd better warn Mom." I hadn't even thought about how my parents would handle this news.

"Why are you here?" I ask him again. "I thought you were rusticating on your farm."

"Do you remember Jerry Brinker?"

"The movie producer?"

"That's him. He's looking to start a hockey team, and he wants me to help decide the best place to do that." Mac played for the San Diego Breeze right after college. He trusted me to invest his money and I put it into crypto along with mine. As such, he doesn't have to work if he doesn't want to.

"Doesn't California already have enough NHL teams?" I ask him.

"Yeah, but everyone is talking about how Mexico is the next big thing in hockey. We're thinking of looking there or maybe even as close by as Santa Barbara." He shrugs. "I thought it might be fun to be part of a team again."

"Are you going to play?" Mac officially retired a couple of years ago. He claimed not to like all the politics, but the truth is, I think he was tired of living on someone else's schedule.

"No way, my team days are over. I just want to be in the mix without taking any more pucks to the side of the head."

"So, you'd be a part owner?"

"A small part. I don't want any of the hassle of management or anything."

I laugh. While Mac and I are twins, he's way more laid back than I've ever been. Even though we both have enough money to last ten lives, I still like to work. My brother likes to dabble. "So, you called to see if you could stay here?" I ask.

He scoffs. "I *know* I can stay here. I called to ask if you wanted a piece of the new team?"

"Not in a million years," I tell him. "Once I leave Maple Falls, I'm done with hockey." I spend the next hour regaling him with stories about the Ice Breakers, the town, and even Ellie. Then I suggest, "Why don't you ask Troy?"

"I already did. He said he's got enough on his plate." Eyeing me closely, he says, "Tell me about this Ellie."

I don't even try to play it cool. "She's amazing. She lives in Maple Falls and takes care of her sick mom. She's a skating instructor and Troy and Kelly's all-around helper. She's beautiful and kind and feisty ..."

Mac laughs. "You've got it bad, man."

Nodding my head, I agree. "And at the worst possible time."

"You mean with Yolanda getting ready to tell the world she's going to have your baby?"

I practically roar in frustration that this is my life. Pulling my phone out of my pocket, I quickly check for messages and find one from Ellie. Standing up, I tell my brother, "I've got to make a call. In the meantime, check the kitchen drawer for takeout menus and order us some supper."

"Why don't we just go out?" he wants to know.

"Because no one can know I'm here. I need the world to think I'm still in Maple Falls."

Walking into the house, I head toward the primary bedroom. As much as I love spending time at the beach, the sound of the surf is so loud, you can't hear anyone on the other end of a call when you're outside. I tap the button to connect me to Ellie and wait while the phone rings.

"Hello?" Her voice is breathy like she's just sprinted a mile.

"It's me," I tell her.

"Zach." Just the sound of her saying my name sends waves of warmth through me.

"How's your mom?"

"She's mad about being in the hospital. She'll be there for a couple more days."

"Tell her hello for me," I say before asking, "How was breakfast with Yolanda?"

She's quiet for so long I start to get nervous. She finally says, "I'm torn."

"About what?"

"Yolanda says you're the father of her baby."

"She's already telling people?" I nearly fall onto the bed at the thought that it might be too late to convince people I'm innocent.

"So you don't deny it?" Ellie's voice sounds strained.

Wait? What? Does she believe Yolanda? "Of course I deny it. I told you I never so much as held hands with the woman." When she doesn't answer right away, I demand to know, "Have you changed your mind about me?"

Instead of answering, she says, "Yolanda knows what an amazing kisser you are."

"First of all, she knows no such thing, and secondly, you think

I'm an amazing kisser?" As hurt as I am that she's doubting me, I can't help but tease her.

She quietly responds, "You know you are."

"A kiss is only as good as the investment of both of the people participating in it," I tell her.

Her mood seems to lighten as she asks, "So you think *I'm* an amazing kisser?"

"Oh yeah," I tell her. "I haven't been able to stop thinking about kissing you."

"Zach." She's back to sounding serious. "I want to believe you, but I'm afraid."

"Of what?"

"Of being hurt. Of being left behind. I'm not a big risk taker and liking you is a huge risk."

I try to put myself in Ellie's position and I guess I can see her point. "I thought we'd agreed to take things one day at a time. If we do that, then surely the risk won't feel so big."

"Says a man who isn't risking anything."

I stretch out on the bed and stare at the raging surf outside my window. "Of course I'm risking something. I'm risking my heart." Before she can respond, I add, "We both have to trust our instincts, Ellie. It's the only way."

I hear her take several breaths before she finally says, "Okay."

"Okay, what?" I need to hear her say the words.

"Okay, I'll trust my instincts."

"And what are they telling you?" *Come on, Ellie, believe in me.*

"That you're telling the truth. But you should know that I was full of doubts earlier this morning and I told Yolanda you're staying at the cottage." Before I can comment, she asks, "You still are, aren't you? I haven't seen your car here all day."

"I'm in Malibu," I tell her. I don't care what Tony says. If Ellie is willing to trust me, I have to be willing to trust her.

"Why?"

"The man who owns the PR agency I use has a plan."

"Doesn't that agency also rep Yolanda?" She sounds worried.

"They do, but they're going to cut ties."

"What's the plan?"

"I don't know yet. All I know is that he wants me out of Maple Falls when Yolanda tells everyone that her baby is mine."

"Zach," Ellie says. "You said that you trust me, right?"

There's something about Ellie that makes me want to believe everything she says, which is not like me. I'm normally a very cautious man. "I've never doubted you."

"Well, then, I might have a plan, too."

"What is it?" Even though I trust Ellie, I'm not sure manipulating the press is a talent she possesses.

"Give me a little bit of time," she says. "Tell your PR guy you have someone working on your behalf here in Maple Falls."

"And if your plan doesn't work?" I ask.

"Then we'll weather the storm together, Zach. Because I believe in you, and I also believe the truth wins out. We won't let Yolanda have the final say here."

And while I'm not quite as optimistic as Ellie, I like the idea of her and me against the world. I know the kind of woman she is, and I can't believe my luck that she's standing by me. "Okay," I tell her. "But just so you know, I can't wait to come back to Maple Falls and kiss you again. For hours."

As much as I want to get rid of Yolanda, Ellie really has become my biggest focus.

CHAPTER TWENTY-EIGHT

Ellie

I know Zach is hurt that I didn't believe him—even for a short time, but I'm glad he's not holding it against me.

After hanging up with him, I call Yolanda. "Can you meet me for a drink tonight?"

"I can't really drink in my condition." She sounds annoyed.

"Meet me for milkshakes at the diner on Maple Falls Road," I tell her. "I have an idea that might just bring Zach to his knees."

Her excitement becomes obvious. "I'll be there at seven."

Looking at the clock, I realize it's already quarter 'til seven, so I grab my car keys and run out of the house.

Shirley May waves at me as soon as I walk into the diner. "I hope you're meeting the big tipper."

"Not tonight, I'm afraid. But I promise to bring him in soon."

She laughs. "If you do, tell him to tip like a normal person. I nearly had a coronary the other day."

"I'll do no such thing," I tell her. "You work for tips, so why not let someone do it right?"

She tilts her head to the side like she's seriously considering the option of not taking easy money, when she finally decides, "Fine. I'll take it. Now, is it just you or are you meeting someone?"

Yolanda walks in, so I point to her. "Just the two of us."

Shirley May acts like she has no idea who Yolanda is, and honestly, she might not. Maple Falls is not used to the kind of celebrity that has descended upon us in recent days.

Leading us to a table, Shirley May says, "I'll give you a couple minutes."

Yolanda looks around with an expression that suggests she just bit into a lemon. "This is *quaint*." I translate that to mean she would never eat in a place like this on her own. Which makes me think even less of her than I already do.

"The food is great," I assure her.

Without looking at the menu, she demands, "What's your plan?"

Before I answer, I wave to Shirley May and order two strawberry milkshakes and a basket of onion rings. Once she's gone, Yolanda announces, "I can't eat that. I'm about to become a blimp. I don't want to get there ahead of schedule." Her comment is so distasteful it makes me wonder how I ever believed anything she said.

"You're about to get big with a child," I tell her. "That's not the same as getting fat."

"Pregnant fat or real fat, it's all the same on television," she complains. "Now, what's your idea?"

"You want to make sure that when you tell the world you're pregnant, Zach is there. That way, if he denies it, it will make him look bad."

Sounding skeptical, she says, "He hasn't seemed to have minded looking bad up to now."

I call on all my high school acting skills—I played Mercutio in my tenth-grade production of *Romeo and Juliet*—and lie. "Kelly Hart said that Zach is eaten up by all the bad press, and that he'll do anything to end it."

Yolanda looks intrigued. "So, your whole plan is that I have Zach there? That doesn't seem like much of a plan."

I shake my head. "There's more. I think you should be waiting for him in the cottage he's renting with a cameraman. In that setting, it'll look like you're staying with him and that you've reconciled."

Yolanda's expression shifts from suspicion to pure joy. "I like this idea, but I'll need you to let me inside so I can surprise Zach when he shows up."

"Of course," I tell her. "I think you should do it tomorrow."

"Do you know when Zach will be gone?"

"I don't, so you'll have to be flexible," I tell her.

Her head starts moving like a bobble head on a dashboard. "I can do that."

Shirley May comes back with both milkshakes and the basket of rings. As soon as she drops them at the table, Yolanda stands up. "I need to go. I'll call you in the morning." I'm relieved she's leaving. I don't need anyone judging me for the delicious food I'm about to enjoy.

Once she's gone, I pick up the phone and call Zach. "Yolanda is going to announce she's pregnant tomorrow. She's going to do it from your cabin." I explain how she'll have a cameraman with her so she can film Zach's reaction.

"This won't work unless she's filming live," he says. "We can't risk her editing the footage." He pauses for a second before adding, "Let me see if Tony can get another reporter there. One that will make sure the tape airs. The timing might be tight though."

"Let me know and I'll get Yolanda there," I tell him.

"You have to make sure she doesn't suspect anything. We need the element of surprise on our side," he says.

"Whatever reporter your guy finds can stay in my house until Yolanda is in your cabin," I tell him. While I really do think this is a brilliant plan, I realize there are a lot of moving parts and I start to get nervous. Even though I'm trying to figure out how things could backfire, I tell Zach, "With any luck, we might actually pull this off."

"We sure might, Ellie. Let me call Tony. I'll call you back when I have news."

"Okay," I say, but I don't hang up the phone.

"Good night, Ellie," Zach says sweetly.

"Good night."

"Would you have let me kiss you if I was there?"

I release a groan deep in my throat before answering, "Yes."

"Good. I want you to think about that."

I guarantee that will now be the only image in my mind, but I don't tell him that. Instead, I challenge, "Only if you think about me kissing you."

"I haven't been able to think of anything else, and with any luck I'll be able to do it for real in a couple of days."

After hanging up, my mind whirls with all things Zach, until I go to bed a few hours later. I don't actually expect to fall asleep, but the minute I close my eyes, I'm gone. I don't even dream, I just pass out into oblivion and sleep through the night until my phone startles me awake.

"Hello?"

"It's Zach. I'm sorry to call so early."

Sitting up, I ask, "Do you have news?"

"Tony was able to get Melinda Star from *American Wrap*."

"Holy heck, she's big!"

"She is," he says. "She wasn't happy about taking a red eye to Washington from New York last night, but she wants this scoop. She and her camera operator will arrive at your house straight from the airport. She wants you to have Yolanda situated at the cottage by two this afternoon."

Even though my mind is spinning with potential roadblocks, I tell him, "I can do that. Can you get word to Melinda that I'll leave a key to my house under the mat? I'm going to have to stalk Yolanda, so she doesn't show up early and run into them."

"Will do," he says before asking, "Are you nervous?"

"Terrified, how about you?"

"I'm just happy to be getting this all settled before the hockey games start. As much as Troy wanted me there to ensure a big press turnout, I'd rather not do so with my head on the chopping block."

"Totally," I tell him. "I need to get going. I've got a busy day ahead of me."

"I wish I could be there to help," Zach says.

"I'll keep in touch, so you know what's going on," I tell him.

"Thanks for everything, Ellie. You're an amazing woman."

"I'm looking forward to hearing you say that in person."

"Fingers crossed that's tomorrow," he says in a low, sexy voice before adding, "Good luck."

As I hang up, I realize we're going to need luck. Yolanda Simms is a pro and I'm fairly certain no one catches her unaware —until today, hopefully.

CHAPTER TWENTY-NINE

Zach

I nervously pace around my house for hours until Mac says, "Dude, go for a run or something. You're stressing me out."

"I can't leave until this thing with Yolanda is settled."

"When is that going to be? Because if it's not soon then *I'm* leaving."

Looking at my phone, my heart starts to beat like a drum in a heavy metal rock anthem. I read Ellie's latest text out loud. "Melinda Star is at my house now. Yolanda will arrive in thirty minutes."

"Thank God," Mac says.

Picking up the television remote off the coffee table, I turn on the TV. Keeping it on mute, I tell my brother, "Melinda's segment airs live at three our time."

"You know this could go spectacularly wrong, don't you?" he asks.

I glare at him. "Of course I do." Then I walk out of the room.

Once I'm in my bedroom, I call Ellie. "How's it going?"

"I've been nervous sweating all day," she says. "But Melinda is nice. Way nicer than Yolanda."

"What did you say to get Yolanda there?" I want to know.

"I told her you'd be here at two and that she needed to arrive before then. She has no idea what's about to happen."

"I could have never done this without you, Ellie."

"It's not done yet, Zach. Shoot … Yolanda's here. I've got to go. Just make sure you're watching Melinda's segment." She hangs up without saying goodbye.

Walking back into my living room, I plop down on the sofa to wait. I try to read a book. I try to close my eyes and meditate. I even try counting, but I only get to twenty before I forget what number I'm on. I've never excelled at waiting.

Finally, when I don't think I can take it anymore, the opening music for *American Wrap* starts to play. The anchor, Angus Johns, stares into the camera and announces, "We've all eagerly been watching the drama brew between reporter Yolanda Simms and billionaire Zachary Hart."

He turns to look into another camera before adding, "And folks, things are heating up. Our very own Melinda Star is reporting live from Maple Falls, Washington."

The image on the screen shifts from the studio to the front of the cottage I'm renting from Ellie. Melinda turns to the camera and says, "Good evening, this is Melinda Star reporting from Maple Falls, Washington, with an update to a story that's captivated us all." She knocks on the door before stepping out of the focus of the camera.

When the door opens, Yolanda is standing there wearing nothing more than a towel. *What in the world is she doing?*

"Yolanda Simms?" Melinda asks unnecessarily. We can all see it's Yolanda.

"Melinda?" Yolanda is clearly caught off guard. "What are *you* doing here?"

"I've come to ask some questions about Zachary Hart. I hope this is a good time."

A variety of expressions cross Yolanda's face. There's shock, panic, and then finally a look of pure satisfaction. "Will you give me a minute to put on a robe?"

"Of course," Melinda says.

Yolanda is gone for less than ten seconds before she's back, tying the sash on a red satin robe that looks like it's more for seduction than coverage. Stepping out onto the front porch, Yolanda says, "Zach is inside napping."

Melinda's eyes open wide. "Are you saying that you and Zach are staying here together? I thought things had gone south between the two of you."

Yolanda doesn't even try to hide the look of delight on her face. "Zach and I were waiting to make this announcement, but being that you're here, I might as well tell you that he and I are expecting a baby. We couldn't be more excited."

"You and Zachary Hart are having a child together?" She's clearly shocked.

Yolanda runs her hand over her still-flat stomach and smiles. "We are."

Looking at a pad of paper in her hand, Melinda asks, "And you used the Beverly Hills Fertility Clinic to help?"

Yolanda's knees appear to be on the verge of giving way, which forces her to lean against the door jamb for support. "Why would you think that?"

"Didn't Dr. Felicity Saipan perform in vitro fertilization on you?"

Yolanda is caught so completely off guard I nearly laugh. "It's nobody's business how Zach and I created our child. A lot of women have trouble conceiving."

"They do," Melinda agrees before sharing, "My husband and I went through quite an ordeal to have our children."

Sighing sympathetically, Yolanda says, "So you know how tough it can be."

"I do. But I also know that you can't have in vitro without a form clearly signed by both parents unless you're using a sperm donor."

Yolanda is starting to see the writing on the wall. "Those forms are confidential."

"Of course," Melinda tells her. "But you've already told us that Zachary Hart is the father so I'm sure you won't mind making your form public."

"I … well … I mean …" Yolanda is stuttering like she has lost the ability to speak English.

"I'd love a chance to ask Zach himself." Melinda points into the cottage. "You said he's taking a nap? Would you mind waking him up?"

"I did say that …" Yolanda begins. "But what I meant is that he's just gone out to get supper for us."

"I'll wait," Melinda tells her.

That's clearly not what Yolanda wants to hear. "Why don't I have him call you when he gets back? He might be awhile."

Melinda momentarily glances at the camera before saying, "But he was just here, right?"

"We were taking a *nap* only thirty minutes ago," Yolanda answers. Her emphasis on the word "nap" clearly suggests anything but sleeping was going on.

Turning fully toward the camera, the reporter from *American Wrap* intones, "That's interesting, Yolanda, because I have it on good authority that Mr. Hart is currently at his beach house in Malibu."

Yolanda's eyes shift from side-to-side nervously. "I assure you Zach is here in Maple Falls."

A knock at my front door causes me to practically hit the ceiling in surprise. Looking at my brother, I tell him, "Our food has arrived."

"I didn't order it yet."

Getting up, I hurry to open the door only to be met by a camera. A local reporter named Henry Hanks is standing there as well. Shoving a microphone in my face, he announces, "Hello, Mr. Hart. I'm just here to prove that you're not in Maple Falls, Washington, right now."

Holy heck. Tony didn't give me any indication this was going to happen. "As you can see, I'm not," I tell him.

"Then I'm guessing you didn't just take a *nap* with Yolanda Simms?"

"Yolanda and I are not a couple. We've never been a couple."

"I think you're telling the truth, Zach," Henry says. "As such, I'm going to go out on a limb and guess you're not her baby daddy."

Pretending I have no idea what he's talking about, I ask, "What baby?"

Henry faces the camera. "And there you have it, folks. It looks like Yolanda Simms has been lying about her relationship with Zachary Hart." He turns to me and asks, "Is there anything you'd like to say to America, Zach?"

Leaning toward his microphone, I tell him, "Only that I've never lied about what's occurred between Yolanda and me. We went out on three dates, but that's all."

"Are you dating anyone else?" Henry wants to know.

I can't stop the grin from forming on my mouth. "I've recently met a very special woman. We've been on one date, but I hope there will be many more to come."

Henry looks startled by my answer, but he still manages to ask. "Would you like to tell us who that person is?"

"Her name is Ellie Butler," I say. "She's a skating instructor in Maple Falls and she's the loveliest woman in the world." I have no idea how Ellie is going to feel about such a public announcement, but I hope she's good with it. These big romantic gestures always seem to work well in the movies.

Henry nods his head. "Thanks for talking to us, Zach. We're happy to finally have the record set straight."

Even though I'm equally pleased, I feel the need to add, "I'm glad the press has finally seen fit to hear both sides of the story."

Henry's face flushes slightly before he tells the camera, "This has been a good lesson for us all. Back to you, Melinda …"

I walk back into my living room to see Mac still watching the

TV. "You looked a bit pale," he says, "But I think your problems with Yolanda are over."

"Thank goodness for that." Picking up my phone, I call Ellie.

Her first words are, "You told everyone about me!"

"Are you mad?" I suddenly worry I might have done the wrong thing.

"No," she says. "I thought it was sweet. Do you mean it? You know, about hoping we're going to become a couple."

"Of course I mean it. Isn't that what you want too?"

"It is," she says quietly. "But I don't know how it's going to work. I still live in Maple Falls and you live in California."

"One day at a time, Ellie. I promise there is no obstacle so big we can't work it out." Then I tell her, "I'm going to be back in town tomorrow. Do you want to have our first official date out in public?"

She surprises me by answering, "I'm not really an out-on-the-town kind of girl. How about if I cook for you tomorrow?"

As if I didn't already know that Ellie wasn't like the other women I've gone out with. Everyone else wants to be photographed with me, and Ellie wants a quiet night in. "That sounds like a great idea," I tell her. "Plus, that way there won't be any prying eyes when I kiss you."

"Or when I kiss you," she practically purrs.

I know without question that Ellie Butler is my future, and I can't wait to experience life with her at my side.

CHAPTER THIRTY

Ellie/Two Weeks Later

"Let's go, Mom!" I call across the house. My mom was cleared by the doctor twelve days ago to resume normal activities. Not only has the brain bleed healed on its own, but the turmeric Zach gave her seems to really be helping with her pain.

I hear the low whirring of her wheelchair before I see her. My mom drives into the living room wearing a pretty summer dress and a smile. "I love this thing!" she says excitedly. Then she sees Zach. "We couldn't have gotten this without you, Zach. Thank you."

"Don't thank me," he says. "Thank your daughter for being a PR mastermind." He smiles in my direction. "Tony asked if you wanted to move to LA and work for him."

I shudder. "I'd rather become a professional mud wrestler."

"Is that a thing?" he asks in horror.

"Who knows. I'm just saying that I never want to be in PR. Especially if it means working for people like Yolanda."

"How about people like me?" he asks with a wink.

Walking over to my purse, I open it and hand him an envelope from inside. He looks confused while opening it. Then he holds up a check. "That's your money back," I tell him.

"I don't want it." He sounds offended.

"I don't either."

"I thought you were going to use it to help with things around here."

"I'm using Yolanda's money for that," I tell him. "I was going to give hers back, too, but I'm so mad at what she's done to you that I've decided to keep it." After a beat, I add, "Although if she asks for it back, I'll probably give her whatever I haven't spent."

Looking at my mom, Zach asks, "Would you like a check for forty thousand dollars?"

My mom shakes her head. "Ellie told me everything, and you can rest easy that neither of us wants your money."

Zach looks like you could knock him over with a feather. "Fine. But I'm paying for everything at Maple Fest today."

"You have yourself a deal," I tell him before sealing our pact with a kiss.

"I knew you two were going to be a perfect match!" my mom cheers.

Zach asks us, "What do you say that after this hockey tournament is over, I take you both to stay at my house on the beach?"

"You don't have ramps," I remind him.

With a wink, he tells me, "I do now. I had my brother hire someone to install them the day I left."

"Don't you think you might be putting the cart before the horse?" I ask.

"What does that even mean?"

My mom injects, "It means, what happens if you and Ellie stop seeing each other?"

"Then I'll have a wheelchair ramp at my house." He hurries to add, "I could start skateboarding."

Even though it's early days, I don't like that Zach's thought about the possibility of us breaking up. I suggest, "You can do that even if we keep seeing each other."

He wraps his arm around me. "That's the real plan. Now, are you two ladies ready to introduce me to the best fall festival this side of the Mississippi?"

"You know it," I tell him while opening the door. I stand back while my mom navigates her travel wheelchair through the opening. We got her a second chair until we can get a car big enough to haul the electric one. Zach follows her out, while I stay back and lock up. My mom stops her wheelchair next to the back door of Zach's SUV, and when I catch up, I help her stand while he puts the travel chair in the trunk.

On the way to the festival, my mom tells Zach, "Maple Fest was Ellie's favorite event during her youth. I think she liked it more than Christmas."

"Christmas didn't come with caramel corn and corn mazes," I complain.

"It should," Zach says. "But personally, I'm hoping to find some apple cider donuts covered in cinnamon sugar."

"Oh, you will," I assure him. "And pumpkin fritters, and pecan tassies, and whoopie pies …"

I could keep going but Zach interrupts. "Will there be real food or just sweets?"

"They'll have brats boiled in beer, Italian sausages, pretzels with cheese sauce, potato pancakes …"

"I should have worn bigger pants," he moans.

"Or we can go back again tomorrow," I suggest.

Zach pulls into the large field by the farmers' market that's being used as a parking lot for Maple Fest. "I'll drop you off up front before finding a spot. What do you say we meet at the donuts?"

"We'll wait for you," I tell him. "It's super crowded and we might not find each other."

Zach pulls over to the entrance and quickly brings my mom's wheelchair around. Once I help transfer her, he leaves to park. "That is one nice man," my mom tells me. "I mean seriously, I don't think you could do better."

A huge smile overtakes my face. "He is pretty terrific. But you know he'll eventually have to go back to LA, and long distance relationships can be tough."

"Good thing he invited us to go with him then," my mom says.

"He invited us to come visit his beach house," I clarify. "That was not an invitation to move."

"While you were locking the front door, he told me the beach house was ours for as long as we wanted it. He mentioned that he hoped we'd stay for a long time."

"Are you seriously telling me that you'd be fine moving to Malibu?" My mother loves Maple Creek.

She shrugs. "Honey, I'm happy being wherever you are. And if you want my opinion, that man is worth following."

I have no idea how to respond to that, so I say, "I don't have a job in LA."

"So, get one."

"I burn easily," I remind her.

"Good thing they make a high SPF sunscreen."

"You would seriously go to Los Angeles on a one-way ticket just so I could be with Zach."

"Honey," she tells me. "I'd go to the moon for you."

My eyes start to fill with tears. When Zach showed up in Maple Falls, I felt like my life was stalled. I was overwhelmed trying to stay on top of my to-do list, which included helping my mom. And now, only a short time later, there are suddenly so many possibilities.

Scanning the crowd inside the entrance my eyes stop on Kiki. I'm about to wave to get her attention when I see who she's talking to. Dan Roberts. There are definite sparks brewing there that I don't want to interrupt. If anyone deserves a happy ending, it's Kiki.

Turning my head, I see Zach cross the parking lot. He jogs up to us and says, "You gals ready to see how much I can eat?"

I lace my fingers through his before giving him a kiss on the cheek. "You're a good guy, do you know that?"

He squeezes my hand. "I must be to have someone like you in my life."

"Get a room!" my mom calls out. Then she laughs. "But feed me first."

Zach and I follow behind her as she navigates her way through the crowd. "My mom said you invited us to move to Los Angeles," I tell him.

"Or I could move here, if you prefer."

I stop dead in my tracks. "You would move to Maple Falls for me?"

"I would," he says. "But I suggest we try out both places before making a final decision."

"Zach, it's only been two weeks since our first kiss. You can't possibly be that sure about us."

He pulls me along as he starts walking. "Part of the reason I'm so successful, Ellie, is because I know a good thing when I see it. And believe me, you and I are great together."

"Let's get through the hockey tournament before we make any decisions," I tell him.

"Fine by me."

"You're seriously that easygoing about this?"

"I seriously am," he says. "That's because I'm serious about you."

If I had to put money on it, I'd bet that in a few short years, Zach and I will not only be married, but we will have started a family. He's right; when you know, you know. Now all we have to do is decide where we're going to live.

GRAB THE NEXT BOOK IN THE SERIES, WHERE KEIRA AND DAN GET THEIR CHANCE, IN:

THE REBOUND PLAY by KATE O'KEEFFE

If you get a second chance at love with your hockey star ex, should you take it?

Keira
What do you do when your NHL superstar ex skates back into your small town? Drop to the ground and hide behind the bleachers, hoping he doesn't see you. But Lady Luck must be in a bad

mood today because Dan spots me, my hood over my eyes, pretending I'm not there.Mature? No.

Necessary? Oh, yes.

Humiliation washes over me, and the wall around my heart stands firm. Dan might be back, but I can't afford to let him in again. Not after the heartbreak of losing him once before.

When he offers to coach my nephew, I reluctantly agree. Every smile he flashes at me, every kind word, threatens to crack my resolve. But I can't go through that again. I have to protect my heart.

Dan
I want Keira back. End of story.

The Rebound Play is a love story about a jock and a nerd who get a second chance in this small town romance with all the sizzle and chemistry, but none of the spice.

YOUR MAPLE FALLS RECIPE: SHIRLEY MAY'S CARAMEL CORN W/ PECANS AND MACADAMIA NUTS

Shirley May's Caramel Corn w/ Pecans and Macadamia Nuts

Ingredients

3 quarts popped corn (use a good quality so you're not biting into un-popped kernels)
1 Cup brown sugar
½ Cup light corn syrup
½ Cup butter
½ teaspoon salt
½ teaspoon baking soda
1 Tablespoon vanilla extract
1 Cup macadamia nuts, coarsely chopped
1 Cup pecans, coarsely chopped

Directions

1. Preheat oven to 250 degrees.
2. Spray two large, shallow roasting pans with cooking spray.
3. Place half the popped corn and nuts into each.

4. In a 4-quart sauce pan, melt butter, sugar, corn syrup, and salt. Stir constantly over medium heat until the mixture boils.
5. Turn heat down and continue to boil without stirring for 5 minutes.
6. Remove from heat and stir in vanilla and baking soda.
7. Pour half of the mixture over each pan and stir until well coated.
8. Place both pans in the oven and bake for an hour, changing the racks every fifteen minutes.

CAST OF CHARACTERS IN THE LOVE ON THIN ICE SERIES

Angel Davis: love interest is Scotty MacFarland; cousins with Harlow Lemieux; collaborates with Emmy Roberts to have books at Happy Horizons Ranch.

Blair Radcliffe: love interest is Cooper Montgomery; best college friends with Keira Johnson; knows Willa Blackwell through work connections.

Cooper Montgomery: love interest is Blair Radcliffe; plays for the Tennessee Wolves; went to college with Ted "The Bear" Powell; knows Scotty McFarland from the minor leagues; right winger, #89.

Dan Roberts: love interest is Keira Johnson; brother of Emmerson Roberts; best college friends with Dawson Hayes; played in the Chicago Blizzard with Troy Hart; nickname is Dan the Man; center, #29.

Dawson Hayes: love interest is Emmy Roberts; college friend of Dan Roberts; played on the Carolina Crushers; goalie, #1.

CAST OF CHARACTERS IN THE LOVE ON THIN ICE SERIES

Ellie Butler: love interest is Zach Hart; friends with Keira Johnson.

Emmy Roberts: love interest is Dawson Hayes; sibling to Dan Roberts; friends with Keira Johnson.

Harlow Lemieux: love interest is Ted "The Bear" Powell; Angel Davis's cousin; friends with Willa Blackwell.

Keira Johnson: love interest is Dan Roberts; best college friends with Blair Radcliffe; friends with Angel Davis, Ellie Butler, and Emmerson Roberts.

Noah Beaumont: love interest is Willa Blackwell; former NHL superstar who now plays for the AHL team, River City Renegades; defenseman, #5.

Scotty MacFarland: love interest is Angel Davis; former player with the Denver Peaks; knows Cooper Montgomery and Ted Powell from minor league days; second coach for Ice Breakers, #14.

Ted "The Bear" Powell: love interest is Harlow Lemieux; plays for the Nebraska Knights; went to college with Cooper Montgomery; defenseman, #58.

Willa Blackwell: love interest is Noah Beaumont; college friend of Harlow Lemieux and knows Blair Radcliffe through work connections.

Zach Hart: love interest is Ellie Butler; billionaire backer of the Ice Breakers; brother of Ice Breakers' founder, Troy Hart.

ALSO IN LOVE ON THIN ICE

Breaking the Ice by Whitney Dineen

The Rebound Play by Kate O'Keeffe

The Friend Face-Off by Grace Worthington

Love in Overtime by Melissa Baldwin

The Parent Playbook by Elsie Woods

Love at First Skate by Ellie Hall

Penalties and Proposals by Anne Kemp

AVAILABLE NOW: PITY DATE

If you love small-town romcom, check out Whitney's Pity Series starting with *Pity Date* (over 1600 5-star reviews on Amazon!).

A week ago, if you told me my boyfriend was cheating on me, I would have called you a liar.

If you said a movie star would walk into my bakery and offer to help make my ex jealous, I would have thought you'd eaten one too many of the special brownies the old folks in town are talking about.

And if you had the audacity to suggest my fake date would turn into the love of my life? I would have told you to stop toying with me. I've been through enough disappointment lately.

There's no way a movie star is going to fall in love with a bakery owner from Wisconsin. This isn't a Hallmark movie.

But I'm starting to wish it was …

Grab your copy of Pity Date today!

ABOUT THE AUTHOR

USA Today Bestseller Whitney Dineen is a rock star in her own head. While delusional about her singing abilities, there's been a plethora of validation that she's a fairly decent author (AMAZING!!!).

After winning many writing awards and selling nearly a kabillion books (math may not be her forte, either), she's decided to let the voices in her head say whatever they want (sorry, Mom). She also won a fourth-place ribbon in a fifth-grade swim meet in backstroke. So, there's that.

Whitney loves to play with her kids (a.k.a. dazzle them with her amazing flossing abilities), bake stuff, eat stuff, and write books for people who "get" her. She thinks french fries are the perfect food and Mrs. Roper is her spirit animal.

Join her newsletter for news of her latest releases, sales, and recommendations. If you consider yourself a superfan, join her private reader group, where you will be offered the chance to read her books before they're released.

ALSO BY WHITNEY DINEEN

Pity Series

Pity Date

Pity Party

Pity Pact

Pity Parade

Pity Present (Coming Soon)

The Mimi Chronicles

The Reinvention of Mimi Finnegan

Mimi Plus Two

Kindred Spirits

Relatively Series

Relatively Normal

Relatively Sane

Relatively Happy

Creek Water Series

The Event

The Move

The Plan

The Dream

Seven Brides for Seven Mothers Series

Love is a Battlefield

Ain't She Sweet

It's My Party

You're So Vain

Head Over Feet

Queen of Hearts

At Last

She Sins at Midnight

Going Up?

Love for Sale

The Accidentally in Love Series (with Melanie Summers)

Text Me on Tuesday

The Text God

Text Wars

Text in Show

Mistle Text

Text and Confused

A Gamble on Love Mom-Com Series (with Melanie Summers)

No Ordinary Hate

A Hate Like This

Hate, Rinse, Repeat

Conspiracy Thriller

See No More

Non-Fiction Humor

Motherhood, Martyrdom & Costco Runs

Middle Reader

Wilhelmina and the Willamette Wig Factory

<u>Who the Heck is Harvey Stingle?</u>

Children's Books

<u>The Friendship Bench</u>

www.ingramcontent.com/pod-product-compliance
Lightning Source LLC
Chambersburg PA
CBHW020959180626
46814CB00003B/1169